HE
DONE
HER
WRONG

HE
DONE
HER
WRONG

A TOBY PETERS MYSTERY
BY STUART M. KAMINSKY

ST. MARTIN'S PRESS
NEW YORK

Library of Congress Cataloging in Publication Data

Kaminsky, Stuart M.
  He done her wrong.

  1. West, Mae—Fiction.   I. Title.
PS3561.A43H4   1983   813'.54   82-16912
ISBN 0-312-36491-1

First Edition

10 9 8 7 6 5 4 3 2 1

For Aunt Sylvia and Uncle Joe

Nellie knows people are divided into the goods and the bads. The thing is not to be caught with the goods.

—Mae West, *The Pleasure Man*

CHAPTER 1

The best-looking Mae West in the room, outside of Mae West herself, was a Chinese guy named Richard Hom who wanted to be a comedian. I counted no less than forty Mae Wests in the room, at least one of whom was a thief.

I met Mae West the last day in April 1942, a cool day with no sun. I had called her number the day before, after talking to my brother Phil, and a man had answered and told me to come out the next morning. The man then told me how to get to her ranch in the San Fernando Valley, and I told my mechanic, No-Neck Arnie, that he had to turn all his magic on to keep my '34 Buick going a few more days. He had taken half my last fee to repaint the car and fix the dents an angry elephant had made in it.

"Oliver ain't gonna make it through the summer," Arnie had said, shifting his cigar to the other side of his mouth and rubbing the new black paint job. "You shouldn't sink any more gelt into it. I tell you for a fact." It bothered me that Arnie had named the car Oliver, since I always thought of it as a female.

"I can't afford a new car," I explained. "Inflation is here, Arn. My income is low. Cars are hard to get. The war."

He wiped his greasy hands on his greasy overalls, spit on the roof of Oliver where he saw or imagined he saw a taint in the paint, and rubbed his sleeve on it professionally.

"I know a guy can get you a '38 Ford coupe for two hundred cash and no questions," he said. "Runs good."

"If I get two hundred, I'll be back."

"Suit yourself," he shrugged in a not-too-bad imitation of Randolph Scott.

I suited myself and headed for the valley. The car sounded fine most of the way. Instead of listening to it or the radio, I went over what I had picked up from the *L.A. Times'* files the night before. The few private detectives and all the cops I know claim to have friends at the newspapers in town, reporters or editors who do favors and get favors back. I've got no such contacts. There's not much I can offer besides a little inside information on a few stars, and I make whatever living I've got by keeping my mouth shut.

When I was a kid back in 1925, a Jewish gangster named Dave Berman became a minor folk hero by refusing to testify against his friends in a kidnapping case. "Hell, all they can give me is life," he said, and the kids back in Glendale and across the country picked it up as a catchphrase. For me it was more than that. Berman may have been a kidnapper, but he had something to sell, loyalty and nerve.

I was dressed right for the meeting, a new 100 percent all-wool tropical worsted gray suit I'd picked up from Hy's Clothes for Him for $22.50 new. Four more bucks got me an extra pair of pants. The tie was a striped blue thing I'd been given for my birthday back in November by my friend and next-door neighbor at Mrs. Plaut's Boardinghouse, Gunther Wherthman.

Driving down Laurel Canyon Road, I saw a sign reminding me to CONSERVE FOOD, so I stopped at a little neighborhood market, picked up a dozen eggs for thirty cents, three Lifebuoy soaps for seventeen cents, and a box of spoon-size Shreddies for which I didn't ask the price. Some things are essential even in inflation. With the groceries safely in the trunk, I continued out beyond the cluster of valley towns and into the country roads at the foot of the mountains.

Mae West, according to the guy at the *Times* I had to bribe to let me see the files, was pushing fifty and pulling down maybe three hundred thousand dollars for each movie she wrote and acted in. She was in the middle of a divorce from a guy she hadn't seen in twenty years. She'd been under a lot of pressure from groups claiming she was a bad moral influence, and she hadn't made a movie in two years; but that one, *My Little Chickadee,* according to the *Times* morgue guy, who looked like the paper in his files—fragile, old, and a little yellow—had earned a pile of money for Paramount.

That was enough to know and think about until I got some facts. I flipped on the radio and picked up Connie Boswell singing "Stardust." I hummed along with her till I found the road I'd been directed to just outside La Canada and urged Oliver to pull us by the retreads up to the big two-story house. Mae West didn't live in the middle of nowhere—she lived on its fringes.

The whole thing had started a week earlier when my brother Phil had cornered me in my office, a cubbyhole with a door inside the dental suite of Sheldon Minck, D.D.S.

Phil is a few months from his first half century on earth. His hair is steel gray to match his disposition and his body solid, with more than a hint of cop gut. Both of which are appropriate, since he is a Los Angeles Homicide lieutenant hoping, in spite of the people he has antagonized over the years by failing to control his temper, to make captain in the near future. Phil is angry about criminals. No matter how many he has stomped, kicked, threatened, and maimed, no matter how many he has railroaded, goaded, and locked up with questionable evidence and the real thing, there are always others to take their place, always more than the week before. Phil strikes with outrage at crime, but there are moments when he focuses some of that hatred on me.

He has been doing that for a lifetime, too. It is his therapy. At home he is a gentle father and a tender husband. He has to be. His wife, Ruth, looks like a finely shaved toothpick ready for exhibition at the "Believe It or Not Show." He has to have someone he loves to take it out on.

So, I was surprised to find him in my office that afternoon, asking me for a favor. It was the only thing he had asked me for in his life, and it came hard to him. He love-hated me and I did the same for him, but he trusted me, and this favor took trust.

"Mae West," he had said with a grunt.

Something like silence had settled over my little office, if you discount the sound of Shelly Minck in the next room drilling away on a patient and singing "When the Red, Red Robin Goes Bob, Bob, Bobbin' Along." You also had to discount the various other unidentified sounds of the Farraday Building and Hoover Street outside, but I was pretty good at that. I looked at the cracked wall holding the 1907 photograph of Phil with his arm around me holding the collar of our dog Murphy while our father looked proudly at the both of us. Murph was later renamed Kaiser Wilhelm when Phil came back from the Big War, which had now been replaced by another Big War with some of the same people.

"I want you to do something for Mae West," he said, removing the tie from his thick neck.

"O.K.," I said.

"Don't you want to know what it is before you agree?" he said, looking at me.

"I've agreed. Now tell me what it is."

He laughed a this-is-not-funny laugh.

"I see," he said between teeth that were reasonably straight and clean for someone who spent so much time grinding them together and probably biting suspects. "You think this will give you some edge, make me owe you, give you something you can cash in on later."

"I hadn't thought about it, but I'll consider it a suggestion." I resisted the urge to put my feet up on the desk, one of the four or five hundred habits I have that drive Phil to violence. I remembered the last time he had knocked my feet off his desk at the Wilshire station. It had resulted in my seeing an orthopedic surgeon.

"Toby," he said. "No wise talk or I walk."

"O.K., Phil. Do me a favor? Don't walk. Let me help you. Please. I'll be good."

Phil looked at the ceiling and explained that he had known Mae West when she came to the coast back in 1931. He didn't say how he knew her or how well, but it had been either just before or just after he married Ruth. He didn't make it clear, and I didn't push. They had been friends or *friends,* and she had now called him with a request for help, but it wasn't quite a police matter. Phil had promised to help, and that promise had brought him to my office.

"She wrote a book," he explained, "a life story sort of in fictional form. She had one copy, and it turned out to be missing about a week ago. Gone right out of her apartment in town over near Paramount. It took her a long time to put it together, and it'll take her a couple of years to do it again. She's also worried about someone publishing it as a novel under their name. She can't prove it's hers."

"And," I said, "she wants someone to get it back for her."

"It's more than that," Phil went on. "Some guy called her, offered to sell it back, even told her when he'd make the exchange for five grand. She agreed, but she thinks something's funny about the whole thing. The guy stays on the phone too long, rambles. She thinks he's a nut and a not straight-through-the-window-and-out-the-door gonif."

"And you can't do anything?"

"She wants it kept quiet if possible," he signed. "I owe her be . . . just leave it that way. I owe her. I'm not sure she has enough of a case for me to take it on if she wanted me to do it officially. It sounds too much like a publicity stunt. Well?"

"I said I'd do it," I reminded him.

He got up and reached into his back pocket. Even with sagging pants his rear was large and the pull difficult. He finally extracted a worn wallet and handed me a card from Ruffillo's Bail Bond with a phone number.

"The other side," he said. I flipped it and saw a phone number in pencil and the name *Mae*. I tucked it in my jacket pocket.

Phil started to pull out some five-dollar bills, and I sighed. "Phil." He stopped, jammed the wallet back in his pocket, and moved to the door. He had just finished paying for an operation on one of his kids and was in trouble with his North Hollywood mortgage. He didn't wear the same suit week after week because he looked so good in it.

"Call me if you need my help on this," he said from the door without looking back.

"I'll call."

He almost said thanks. I think he wanted to, but I didn't. You get used to something when you live with it for more than forty years. Our relationship was already in trouble with this visit.

When I pulled in front of Mae West's house, the door opened and two massive guys in their late twenties or early thirties wearing white turtleneck shirts hurried out and set up positions protecting the entrance. I got out and eyed them.

"Hi," I said with my most friendly grin. "My name's Peters, Toby Peters. Miss West is expecting me."

I took a few steps closer and concluded that neither of the two was giving off the spark that signaled intelligence or even animal cleverness. Neither acted as if I had spoken. One was blond. The other had curly black hair. I'd never seen such exaggerated muscles. They looked strangely top-heavy, like Bluto in a Popeye cartoon. They were probably slow, and I could probably take both of them by staying out of their grasp and running a lot. But I had been fooled in the past by those probabilities and wound up more than once (maybe a dozen times if you want a more accurate count) in need of medical help.

"Are you two in there?" I asked, stepping in front of them. "I can come back when you're home."

One of them, the dark one, did something with his full lower lip that could have been a sneer or a smile, or maybe he still had breakfast toast stuck in his perfect white teeth. Since my teeth are neither perfect nor very white, and since I am almost as old as Mae West, I had the urge to push the pair. My world sometimes seems an endless series of encounters with huge men guarding secrets and doors. Each time I meet them I know I have to find out what is beyond that door or go down trying. Hell, the most they can give me is life.

"It's been very nice chatting with you, Dizzy and Daffy," I said, stepping between them, "but I've got some business inside with the lady of the house."

The dark one put an arm out to block me, and I stuck my hand out to push it away. It didn't push. In fact, I almost fell.

"Now all I need is to find the switch to turn you two off." I grinned my most evil grin, but it didn't seem to affect them.

"Your sister eats worms," I tried. No response. "What does it take to get a rise out of you guys?"

"Something you have not got," came a dark voice from the doorway, and out stepped Mae West, but it took me a blink to recognize her. Her voice was the surest touchstone. The woman before me wearing a frilly purple dress had neck-length brown hair, not blond, and was barely on the good side of plump. She gave off a heavy perfume that smelled like a flower I couldn't place and looked at me with amused violet eyes and her hands on her hips.

"Welcome to Paradise," she said, stepping back. "It's a little gaudy and overstocked, but we call it home."

I followed her in with Diz and Daf behind me. A monkey ran across the hallway in front of us, and Mae West nodded. The blond giant hurried after the monkey who had disappeared, heading toward the rear of the house.

"You cut out the tongues of all your servants?" I asked with a smile as she led me into a living room.

"They've got tongues," she said, sitting elegantly in a white chair. "But they use them for better things than idle conversation."

We looked at each other for a few seconds, and I glanced around, waiting for the next verbal game, which I was now convinced I was bound to lose. The room was white and gold. The carpet, drapes, and even the piano were white. The Louis-the-something furniture was gold. She had seated herself beneath an oil painting of a nude reclining. The nude was a somewhat thinner and younger Mae West. The much plumper version was now semi-reclining in the same position with a smile. Dizzy and Daffy had disappeared.

"I don't think I can go on at this level," I said. "I'm used to quiet things like bullets flying, beatings, murders. I came to help, not to lose a verbal match. I know when I'm outclassed."

Her laugh was deep was she sat up and shook her head.

"Sorry," she said. "I've been playing Mae West for so long, I don't know where the playing stops. You want a drink?"

"Sure, Pepsi if you have it."

A few minutes later the blond giant brought in a tray with two drinks. I took the one that was surely Pepsi. She took the dark brown one without the bubbles.

"Steak juice," she explained. "Energy, few calories. Bottoms up."

She drank about half of the juice and then told me her tale. It was pretty much as Phil had set it up. The manuscript was missing. It had been taken not from the ranch but from her apartment at the Ravenswood Hotel near Paramount a few days before.

"He's a real fruit cake," she said, sipping her steak juice. "And I've known some fruits and cakes in my ample career, if you get my meaning."

I got her meaning as she told me that the manuscript contained enough to cause a few scandals.

"It was just a draft," she explained. "I was going to do some cutting, change some names to protect the guilty, though none of it is refragable, and try it out on a few publishers. Now I just want it back, but I think our friendly neighborhood thief is after more than money."

"Like what?" I asked, finishing the Pepsi.

"Even under the circumstances I would like with impudicity to delude myself that I may be the object of his esteem," she said. "But I'm afraid his intentions are strictly honorable. I can read men, and this guy had something destructive on what little is left of his mind."

She had already set up the show for that night and told the thief to come and bring the manuscript. She, in turn, would have an envelope with five grand. The isolated nature of the place, she thought, would make it ideal for keeping him from getting away.

"He's going to be here alone?"

"Not quite," she laughed. "A few of my more intimate friends will be here. We're having a Mae West party. You get in free if you're dressed like me." Her smile was broad, showing teeth that Shelly Minck would have marveled at.

"There's one catch," she added. "Only men are allowed."

"So you're going to have a houseful of men dressed like you, and I'm supposed to find the one who's the thief and nail him?"

"You got it," she said, plunking down her glass with just a brown residue of steak juice remaining.

"You have parties like this often?"

"Since I came out here," she said. "I like men of all shapes, sizes, and persuasion. I even wrote a play back in '29 called *The Drag*. Cast of forty transvestites. Did pretty well, though we couldn't find a theater to take us in New York."

"Too bad," I sympathized. "Anything else I should know about tonight?"

"Just be prepared for any—thing." I could swear her eyes roamed down my pants. "Now, if you will excuse me, I've got to do my exercises. Rollo will show you to a room where you can listen to the radio, take a nap or a bath, and look at yourself in the mirror till lunch. One final question."

"Thirty bucks a day and expenses," I said, "but this one is on the house."

"Thirty bucks a day it'll be," she said. "I don't take things on the house. The house always decides it wants payment in trade. Besides, that wasn't the question."

"Sorry," I said, rising with her. She looked deeply into my eyes as she stepped in front of me.

"How is Phil doing?"

"He's a cop with a family, a lot of bills, and a big stick."

"I know all about the big stick," she said.

"He uses it to break heads," I said. "Like Teddy Roosevelt."

She shrugged and walked slowly out of the room. With her departure the temperature dropped suddenly and the monkey came scurrying in. He was a small thing who paused to show his teeth when I reached down to bar his way. I changed my mind, and massive Rollo came lumbering in pursuit.

The rest of the day I checked out the grounds, made one important phone call, and listened to Dizzy and Daffy galumphing after the monkey. I leafed through a book on yoga, one on life after death, and another by Sigmund Freud.

Sometime early in the evening, the first guests began to arrive. I tightened my tie, put on my jacket, and came out to see what was happening. The first Mae Wests were fair to middling imitations. The real Mae West was pretty good in her blond wig, a tight dress, and a floppy yellow hat with a white feather.

My own invited guest arrived after the first batch, and I placed him where he might be most helpful and least conspicuous.

By nine the place was full of Mae Wests, and Dizzy and Daffy were busy serving drinks and sandwiches. Each guest who didn't know was told the rules: no smoking and no groping.

Just before ten I made my way to the real West, who was holding court on the triumphs of Catherine the Great.

"I was born for that role boys," she said to the assembled group, resembling nothing that could pass for "boys." They nodded in agreement as she excused herself and joined me in a corner.

"Well," I whispered.

"Nothing yet," she sighed. "I've got the envelope up my sleeve and maybe something else too." Her eyebrows went up suggestively.

"Don't you think about anything else?"

"Not in public," she said, reaching up to touch what was left of my nose. "Remind me to ask you sometime how you got that proboscis." She sauntered away on the arm of a tall, thin Mae West who had trouble walking on his white high heels.

The contact came just before midnight, and I almost missed it. The Chinese comic who wanted to be discovered by Mae West, Richard Hom, was telling me about the fight the Chinese were putting up against the Japanese somewhere in Manchuria. It was hard to take him seriously in his costume, but he was serious. So was the signal across the room from Mae West. I pushed away from Hom and made my way through a sea of girdles.

"I've got the book," she said, holding it up. "He's got the money. Said he wasn't through with me. Left by the back door."

"What's he look like?" I said, anxious to move.

"Like me," she said. "A bit too much makeup, and he hasn't got the voice down. Frilly dress, gold with—"

I was off toward the rear. I knew who she meant. I had spotted the guy earlier. He had looked a bit strange—darting blue eyes and a white beaded purse big enough to hold a manuscript or a packet containing five thousand bucks. But since everyone in the place looked strange, I had filed him away. Now I was after him.

I danced past a short Mae West who was saying, "Sure I'd do a Gene Autry, if the price was right," and skipped down the hall.

There was no one in the back rooms. I went through the kitchen where Dizzy and Daffy were busily making little sandwiches. The monkey was in a cage on the kitchen table chattering at his captors.

"Someone just go through here?" I said.

The blond one nodded and the monkey showed his teeth. I went out. There was a slight rain falling, so the sky didn't give me much help. The kitchen window light didn't penetrate very far, but the sound of someone moving through nearby bushes gave me a good idea of the direction I wanted. I plunged in, feeling the new suit tear as I pushed through the shrubs. Whoever was ahead heard me coming and took off. I followed the sound and remembered the layout. He was heading for the pool out back. I leaped over the bushes, falling on my face, got up and ran to head him off.

By the time I hit poolside, the rain was coming down heavily and pinging off the tile edges. Two lights showed the clear bottom of the pool, and I huddled behind a bamboo table and chairs as the sound of someone coming through the bushes grew louder. I could hear someone panting and, I could swear, humming "Three Blind Mice."

When the figure stepped into the clearing in front of the pool, I made my move.

"Hold it right there," I said showing my .38 automatic.

Holding it right there was a rain-soaked figure in a wilting hat. Even in the lack of light I could see he was grinning, which gave me a chill the rain couldn't accomplish. What the hell did he have to grin about? He'd just been caught.

"Just step forward a few feet very slowly."

As he stepped forward, I moved around the pool, wiping rain from my eyes. His makeup was running and I had the feeling I was watching some horror movie or seeing an episode of "Lights Out" come to life. The monster's face was melting, but the monster was smiling.

"Now," I said gently, "just drop the bag and keep on coming with yours hands up." He came. We were about ten feet apart at the edge of the pool when he hissed and dropped the bag.

"I take it," he said in a high-pitched Mae West imitation, "that this means we are not friends."

"You've got a sense of humor," I grinned back. "I like that in a nut with a foot on his throat. Now, we're just going to walk very slowly back to the house."

He didn't move.

"Who are you?" he said, staring at me through soggy mascara. I was sure he had switched to a W. C. Fields imitation.

"Name is Peters," I said. "Private detective. Who are you?"

It was pouring and our voices were muffled. He didn't answer. The chill hit me and I yelled, "Let's move."

He didn't move.

"You want to get shot in drag?" I shouted. "Move. This is a gun. It shoots real bullets and makes holes in people."

He didn't move. I shot twice well over his head into the rainstorm, but he still didn't move. He had me. It was either shoot him or find some other way to bring him in. He turned his back on me and stooped to pick up the purse.

I shoved the gun back into my holster under my soaking jacket, leaped for him and slipped, just managing to grab his stockinged ankle before he reached the purse. He went off-balance, fell on his back, and kicked at me with a spiked heel. The heel caught me on top of the head and his voice, this time as Cary Grant, said, "That will be just about enough of that Mr. Peters, if you please."

He kicked me again, but I held on as he tried to back away by sliding in the grass on his behind.

"I'm taking you in," I said, receiving another kick that caught my neck.

"We are definitely not friends," he said, continuing Cary Grant.

I punched at him as he backed away and hit his kneecap, causing as much damage to my knuckles as his knees. We both groaned.

I thought I had him. Getting to my feet, I stood over him and reached down to grab his wrist as he arched his back and threw another kick. The kick missed but I slipped, backing away, and tumbled into the pool. When I came to the surface, he, she, or it was there to take a swipe at me with the high-heeled shoe. The swipe caught me over the ear, and I went down, gathering what was left of my strength to get out. I made it in about a thousand strokes with the rain trying to push me under. A soaked wool suit didn't make it easier.

As I touched the rim of the pool, something stung my hand. He had circled the pool and was pounding my hand with the shoe.

In addition to my face, health, and reputation, I was about to lose my life. I let go and pushed back into the pool. Through the water I could see the figure, dripping, holding the shoe and drumming it into his palm, waiting for me to make my next try. Half drowned, I let myself drift back to the other side, knowing what would be waiting for me but having no choice. I managed to kick my own shoes off and drop my gun, which gave me a little hope for the far shore.

I had always wanted to go out by way of a bullet, a beating, or, at worst, a free flight from the top of a medium-size building. This bad joke, however, seemed somewhat right for me. I waited for the next blow, but it never came.

Instead I felt myself being lifted out of the water. Either I had died going across the pool, or the only person I knew in the world who was strong enough to lift a fully clothed, 160-pound soaking wet, dead weight out of a pool had turned up.

"Toby, are you alive?" came the voice of Jeremy Butler in my ear. I had stationed the former pro wrestler and present poet at the front drive of the West house to keep the thief from getting away, but something had brought him to my rescue.

"Alive," I gasped. I opened my eyes and looked into his craggy face, enjoying the popping of raindrops off his bald head. "Purse. Money."

"I've got it," he said.

I looked toward the other side of the pool. The thief who had tried to kill me was still there.

"I'm one of the engineer's thumbs," the thief shouted.

Right, I thought. You're an engineer's thumb with a few screws loose in the locomotive.

"Get him," I said.

Jeremy set me down gently, handed me the purse, and ran for the far end of the pool. I slumped down and watched, trying for air. By the time he had reached the corner, the voice of Lionel Barrymore had warned me that "you are on the list now, Peters. On the list."

He was gone into the rain and trees before Jeremy could get to him, but Jeremy followed him into the darkness. I lay there, letting the rain hit my face.

From in front of the house the sound of a starting car engine crashed through the storm. I clutched the purse to my chest and turned my head. A half-dozen dripping Mae Wests were walking toward me. The thief, I thought, had multiplied and returned to finish me off. Then I saw Jeremy break through the sextet.

"Got away," he said.

"I've got an itch that tells me I'd better find him or he'll find me," I gasped. Then I passed out, still clutching the white purse to my chest.

The party was over when I woke up. Actually the night was over, too, and the sun was shining into the room at Mae West's where I had been gently put to bed by Jeremy, who sat in a corner reading a book. I was wearing a pair of purple silk pajamas several dozen sizes too big, probably Dizzy or Daffy's.

"Jeremy."

He put his book away and moved to the bed. He was still dressed in the black sweater and pants of the night before.

"Doctor saw you last night," he said. "He was one of the guests. Said you would probably be all right, but that you should go in for X rays today. I'll drive you."

"No X rays," I said, sitting up with all the pain of a hangover. "I'm afraid of what they'll find in the past. Besides, I've had more X rays than are good for a person in one lifetime."

"The arrow that kills one often comes from one's own arrow sheath," he said.

"What does that mean?" I asked, reaching for his arm to help me up.

"An African proverb," he said, helping me. "I've been studying African poetry. When the war ends, I think there will be a great deal of poetry from Africa."

"My pants," I said. He handed them to me, torn and only enough left of them to cover me till I got home. The jacket was a crumpled mess.

"Shoes are still a little soggy," he said. "Gun is in your glove compartment. I got it from the pool, cleaned and oiled it."

I took off the pajamas but hadn't started to dress when Mae

West came in wearing a purple silk robe with big white flowers on it. She didn't hesitate or even turn her head at the sight of a naked private eye.

"The world has used you for one big punching bag," she marveled. "I've never seen a body like that."

"I'm leaving it to Walter Reed Hospital for research on human abuse."

"I'll bet each one of those scars tells quite a story," she said, crossing her arms and leaning back against the door. "I can see you're no gymnophile."

Too tired for modesty, I gave up on the idea of locating my shorts and painfully pulled on my trousers.

"Half of them were presents from Phil," I grunted, putting on my shirt and crumpled jacket. "The rest are souvenirs."

"The ones on your stomach?" she said.

"In one side, out the other. One is the gift of a woman who will remain nameless, and the other from a crooked Chicago cop I don't want to talk about."

I slumped back against the bed, and Jeremy reached down to grab my arm in case I fell. Mae West stepped forward to help.

"I want to extend my thanks," she said, "and whatever else you might want extended."

"Now now," I said, taking a few deep breaths. "How about thirty bucks expenses and the cost of a new suit, twenty-two-fifty."

"Done," she winked.

"Nope," I said, trying to stand and finding that I could actually manage it. "Don't think this is going to be done till we cage that nut. He said something about a list. Do you know what he was talking about?"

"Haven't the slightest," she said, letting her robe open slightly.

"Said he was an engineer's thumb," I went on.

Both Mae West and Jeremy looked blank.

"Never mind. I have a feeling he'll find us." I took a few steps and found that it was possible. "I think I'll drive back to L.A. with Jeremy. Can you have someone bring my car and drop it at my place?"

"One of my boys will do it," she said.

"Thanks."

"My pleasure. Come back and see me sometime."

I looked at her from the doorway.

"You really use that line."

"Thought it would give you something to tell the boys about," she laughed.

"I'll be in touch," I said as we made it through the house to the distant chattering of the monkey.

My brain proved it was still connected when I remembered to tell Jeremy to pull the groceries out of my trunk. I dozed off during the ride back to Hollywood, where Jeremy got me to my room on Heliotrope without being spotted by my landlady Mrs. Plaut. He deposited me gently on the mattress on the floor. The mattress was there to give added support to my back, which first went out in 1938 when I was given a bear hug by a massive Negro who was annoyed because I tried to keep him from getting to Mickey Rooney at a premiere.

I thanked Jeremy, convinced him to leave me, and looked around the room to be sure it was there and I was still alive. The sofa with Mrs. Plaut's white doilies was within reach, and I could see the table with three chairs, the hot plate, sink, small refrigerator, rug, the purple blanket I was lying on with *God Bless Us Every One* stitched in pink, and the Beech-Nut gum clock I got once as payment for returning a runaway grandma to a guy who owned a pawnshop on Main.

The other boarders were probably at work. I woke to hear the patter of small feet outside my door. The door had no lock. Mrs. Plaut didn't like them.

"Toby?" came a slightly high voice with a distinct accent.

"Come in Gunther," I said, not trying to sit up.

Gunther came in. He is a little more than three feet tall, Swiss, and speaks a dozen or so languages. Always nattily attired, Gunther sits in his room translating foreign books into English for clients ranging from the government to publishing houses.

"You are injured again," he observed, standing over me.

"I am injured, Gunther," I agreed. "Beaten in a swimming pool by a guy dressed like Mae West."

"I see," he said. Gunther had no sense of humor. Some of our best conversations concerned my attempts to explain the humor of something he was trying to translate.

"I'll make some coffee."

While he bustled and put away the few groceries I had picked up, I tested my body. He took out the box of Shreddies, a bowl, and the last of a bottle of milk. I love cereal. Picked it up from my old man who'd get up in the middle of the night for a bowl. Last time we got together before he died back in 1932, the old man and I talked over a bowl of Little Colonels. We talked about the supermarkets that had driven his small Glendale grocery out of business. We talked about my brother and about how I hadn't become a lawyer.

"Ready," announced Gunther. I got up slowly and walked with some strength to the table. I was wearing a pair of boxer shorts and no shirt. Gunther did a reasonably good job of hiding his disapproval, but not good enough. I tested my legs again, made it to the closet, put on a white shirt with only slightly frayed cuffs, and struggled into a pair of cotton pants.

"Gunther," I said, walking to the table where I dropped three large spoons of sugar on my cereal. "The madman I met last night was talking nonsense or giving me a clue. He said something."

Gunther nodded and carefully sipped his coffee without leaning over.

"Something," he repeated.

"Said he was an engineer's thumb."

"Yes," said Gunther, putting down his cup.

"Yes, what?" I asked, pouring the milk and digging in with a spoon. The milk was threatening to turn sour.

"I have translated a story of this name," he said. "Into Polish for a publisher. It is a Sherlock Holmes story."

"O.K. So how can someone be an engineer's thumb?"

He touched his small lower lip and thought seriously while I finished off my cereal and coffee and had another round of both.

"I shall make some inquiry and attempt to answer that question," he said, dabbing his unstained mouth with a paper napkin. He excused himself with dignity, indicating that he would be back to clean up for me.

I did the cleaning up while he was gone, though I knew he preferred to do it himself.

By the time I had dragged myself to the community bathroom down the hall, allowed fifteen minutes for the water to trickle in, bathed, and made it back to my room, Gunther was waiting for me. He was rewashing the dishes.

"Ah, Toby," he said, turning the water off and facing me. "I have discovered your mystery. The Engineer's Thumbs is a Sherlock Holmes group that meets monthly at the Natick Hotel. The current president is a man named Lachtman, an insurance claims adjuster for First Federal of California. All this I learned from an editor who used to be a member of this group."

We sat around talking about the world for an hour or so before Gunther excused himself to get back to work. I headed for the hall phone with the change I could muster to try to track down Lachtman and maybe move a few steps closer to the madman who had tried to kill me and whose list I was on.

CHAPTER 2

The upside-down name card on his tweed sport coat said he was Alvin Aardvark. He stood about six feet tall, weighed a little too much, had thin, washed-out red hair, and a grin full of oversize teeth.

"My name's Randisi, Lou Randisi," he said, taking my hand and pumping it twice. "This is just a joke." He looked down at his name card and let out about an inch more of smile.

"Funny," I said.

He shrugged and looked around the room, probably searching for a lampshade to stick on his head or a small palm tree to dump on the host.

"You're a private detective," he told me.

"Right." I nodded as if he had done a brilliant piece of detection and took a gulp of my Pepsi.

Aardvark said it was to be his pleasant duty to introduce me, and for that he needed a little information. Since I was after some information myself, I thought this might turn into a fair trade.

About a dozen people were in the small dining room at the Natick Hotel in downtown Los Angeles five blocks from my office on Hoover and Ninth.

The Natick was once the most fashionable hotel in the city. The eroded marquee over the First Street entrance, the thin arched windows, and the base of the hardwood staircase with little globe-light standards represented Victorian elegance. A grilled iron elevator cage rose from the center of the large lobby.

The mile stretch of Main Street outside the hotel to Sixth,

known as Calle Principal even in the Mexican days, now consisted of a line of bars, honky-tonks, barber colleges, tattoo shops, pitchmen, pawnshops, flophouses, and all-night dime movies serving as dorms for audiences of bums who slept through movie after movie ignoring the sound.

The decay of most of the street's buildings was accented by their withering Victorian ornamentation. Things were getting better, the war was bringing money that translated into a few improvements, but you could still count on the barrooms sporting yellowed lithographs of Custer's Last Stand on their spotted walls.

It was the monthly meeting of the Engineer's Thumbs, the Sherlock Holmes group, and I was the guest speaker, a real-life detective. Most of the dozen members were women beyond my forty-five years. A few were men. Both men and women glanced at me cautiously but didn't come over to talk. I watched the door to check when each new member arrived; I didn't want to miss my lunatic. It was hard to do that and pay attention to Alvin Aardvark, who was gulping down Dewar's and bubbling with enthusiasm.

"Have you always been a private detective?" he asked, holding his drink away from his jacket while he groped with his free hand in his pockets for something, maybe a pencil and paper, which he never found.

"I was not, like the Dalai Lama, born into my profession," I said politely. "First I was a kid, little and then bigger, followed by a few years as a Glendale cop, followed by a few years as a studio security guard at Warner Brothers, followed by a few years of poverty and creditors. I figured it was time for me to start following something."

Aardvark took a gulp of scotch, lost an ice cube, and watched it slide toward a corner of the room under the feet of a startled old woman in a black suit.

"I'm a teacher," he volunteered, his eyes looking for the cube. I looked for it too. Maybe we could spend a few happy minutes watching it melt.

"A teacher," I repeated, looking back at the door as a small bald man who looked like Donald Meek came in, accompanied by a good-looking, no-nonsense dark woman. The man was carrying a shopping bag from the May Company.

"Too old for the army," Aardvark said, finishing his drink and touching my arm with a grin. "But I'd join like that, if they'd take me." Like that was a failed finger snap.

"Not me," I said, watching Donald Meek agonize over where to put his shopping bag, until his companion directed him to the small main dining table.

"Me either," agreed Aardvark. "I lied. I lie a lot. Don't mean to. Just comes out that way."

"You've got to practice, I advised him, watching two more old ladies come in. "Takes a lot of practice to be a good liar. May be the most important thing a detective can learn."

"I thought about being a writer once," Aardvark chuckled. I didn't see anything funny in wanting to be a writer. He started to say something else, but a wave of noise from the next room drowned him out. When the sound passed, Aardvark nodded toward the other room. "Political stuff, I think. Bunch of guys with straw hats and pictures on donkeys and elephants. In the middle of a war, still thinking about politics." He shook his head. I shook mine and chewed on an ice cube.

"Can I get you a real drink?" he asked, looking at his empty glass.

"Another Pepsi will be fine," said I. "It's full of calories, like the ads say. One hundred and eighty-five calories of pure energy. More than a lamb chop."

Aardvark looked at my battered face, trying to decide if I was joking.

People a lot sharper than the Aardvark had tried to read my kisser and got nowhere. Mine is a dark face with a flat nose topped with a full head of dark hair generously sprinkled with gray. I stand about five nine and do my best to give the impression that I can take on tigers. It's part of the job. The truth is that my nose has been smashed three times in losing causes. Once by my brother Phil's fist, once by a flight through the windshield of a 1931 Oldsmobile, and once by a baseball thrown by my brother. I sweat too easily, dress too shabbily, and usually can't resist the urge to open my mouth when I should keep it shut.

I smiled at an old lady in a little black hat who had looked my way. My smile scared her, and she turned to the other old lady she was with, but I wasn't to be alone for long. Donald Meek advanced shyly and forced himself to meet my eye. Over his shoulder a possible suspect came in, a block-shaped guy about thirty-five wearing a dark suit, a black cape, a floppy white hat, and carrying a cane. He raised his chin and glanced around the room. He saw me but paused only for the space between two adjacent shots in a film and then moved on. He was a real possible.

"I'm Howard Lachtman," the Donald Meek look-alike said, unsure of whether to hold out his hand for a handshake. Instead, he let it rise slightly. I grabbed it and said I was pleased to meet him. I'd talked to him on the phone the day before, asked him about his group, and received the invitation to come to this meeting and be the speaker.

"We've never had a detective talk to us," he had said. "We have no program set yet outside of Jeff and Angela Pierce showing their prewar slides of London and Dick Campbell giving a report on . . ." His voice had trailed off, unable to remember what Campbell was going to report on.

"Sure," I had agreed. "I'll be glad to."

And now Lachtman stood before me, coming about to my shoulders and clearly uneasy.

"We've never had a real detective talk to us before," he repeated.

"I know," I said keeping up my end of the lively art of conversation, which had all the signs of turning into the scene from *To Be or Not to Be* with Jack Benny and Stanley Ridges and Sig Ruman repeating the So-they-call-me-concentration-camp-Erhardt line.

"Why do you call yourselves the 'Engineer's Thumbs,'" I asked, not giving a damn and trying not to lose sight of the caped character who flitted from small group to small group, arching his eyebrows into each conversation.

"Because," Lachtman said, "'The Adventure of the Engineer's Thumb'" is the only Sherlock tale in which the great detective didn't catch the criminal."

I looked around for Aardvark and a fresh Pepsi but couldn't find him.

"Why would you want to name your group after Holmes's only failure?" I asked playing with my now-empty glass.

The question seemed to puzzle Lachtman, who resisted a powerful urge to scratch his hairless head.

"I'm not quite sure. It wasn't my idea. I'll have to ask my wife, Margaritte."

The caped character finally swooped to our duo and, having overheard the last of Lachtman's words, beamed maliciously, put his hand on the small man's shoulder, and uttered in a powerful phony Shakespearean English favored by American drama students, "Is that Officer Margaritte who helps old ladies cross the street?"

Lachtman didn't know how to respond. He grinned weakly and looked in the direction of the woman with whom he had entered, who was busily putting papers on the main table.

"I think I'd better help Margaritte set things up. Dinner will be served soon."

Lachtman eased himself out from under the grasp of the caped man, who allowed his arm to rise majestically. His glance turned to me, and the silver knob of his cane rose to his chin. It looked like a John Barrymore imitation.

"You are the detective."

"That's what the license says," I answered.

He cocked his head dramatically to one side, threw back his cape, and eyed me.

"Do I get the part?" I asked.

"You don't look like a detective," he said grandly and loud enough to take in a few of the old ladies not too far away from us.

"I'm in disguise," I whispered. "Like Holmes. I'm really much taller, far more elegant, and with a voice that's the envy of Harry Marble on the Columbia network news."

"You jest," he said.

"When I can." If he wasn't my madman, he was somebody's.

"We shall see," he said, throwing his cape over his shoulder and turning his back. "We shall see."

It was a great second act closing line for a revival of an old melodrama, but I wasn't sure whether he was referring to my ability to tell a decent joke or to be a detective.

A shout from the politicians next door broke through the walls, and little Howard Lachtman seemed to be getting up enough courage to call our coven to order. I moved toward the door, scaring at least one little old lady Sherlockian, who thought I was coming at her. She gasped and stepped back, proving I hadn't completely lost my charm.

The toilet was behind a pair of wilted palms, and I found myself standing next to a reeling guy wearing a straw hat on a head of corn silk hair. He was grinning and shaking his head as we urinated side by side, the event that has brought men together in philosophical thought since the days of Socrates.

"Political rally?" I asked.

"Salesmen," he answered. "Middle of the worst war in history. Jap troops are at the outskirts of Mandalay. The Russian front is in trouble. The Japs are after Australia, and they announced today that they're drafting 1Bs. I'm 1B, flat feet, bad eyes. And my boss decides it would be a morale builder for the salesmen to have a mock political rally."

He zipped his pants solemnly, steadied himself against the white tile wall, straightened his straw hat, and asked what group I was with.

"Engineer's Thumbs," I said.

"Engineers," he said.

"Right," I agreed, not wanting to make his world any more complicated than it already was.

By the time I got back everyone was seated and waiting for me. There were about twenty of them. Lachtman let out a small sigh when he spotted me and motioned with his hand to the empty seat on his left. I strolled over while the group watched me, and I had the sudden fear that I had forgotten to zip up in the washroom. I settled myself in next to Lachtman, who introduced me to Officer Margaritte.

Lachtman rose and in a far-from-steady voice said that the dinner was about to be served and that the speaker for tonight was Tony Pastor, a real detective who would be introduced more fully later by Lou Randisi. The caped crusader who sat opposite me at one of four round tableclothed tables let his eyes roll upward in anticipation.

Randisi, alias Alvin the Aardvark, sat on my left, hurrying down a scotch.

"Teaching high school is like walking in MacArthur Park. It's nice to look at the animals, but while you're doing it you always step in their crap."

That was the extent of his conversation with me during the meal.

Lachtman kept his head down and attended to eating. Randisi kept his snout in his drink and his mind on his students. It was Friday, May 1, May Day 1942. He had the weekend to look forward to and summer vacation was coming, but it didn't seem to cheer him up through the roast chicken, salad, and orange sherbet.

Lachtman got up to apologize for the lack of sugar for the coffee.

The sale of sugar had stopped three days before and wouldn't begin again till people picked up their sugar ration books on Monday.

"A lot of things are going to be rationed," bellowed the man in the cape, "before this war is over." He looked at Lachtman piercingly, as if the sugar shortage were his fault. Then he said, "Cyril Overton."

I wasn't sure whether that was his name, the person responsible for the shortage, a black-market sugar dealer we could all go to, or someone he was turning the floor over to.

As he sat down, Lachtman said, "'The Adventure of the Missing Three-Quarter.'"

Mrs. Lachtman leaned back to speak over her husband's thin shoulders.

"It's part of our procedure," she explained. "One can throw a challenge from the Canon of Holmes tales and the challenged party must identify the story in which the item appears."

She had good brown eyes and dark hair that reminded me of Anne, my former wife, who was scheduled to marry an airline executive. I smiled at her. She smiled back a bit too officially and returned to her sugarless coffee.

I said something to Aardvark, but he only grunted morosely, staring into his sherbet. He seemed to have a fondness for concentrating on melting things.

When dinner was over, Lachtman pulled some notes from his May Company shopping bag. I could also see a Holmes deerstalker cap in the bag and watched Lachtman's right hand waver over it, almost touch it and pull away. He looked up at his wife, who gave him no sign either way.

"'Darkness,'" she said softly.

"The title of chapter four of 'The Valley of Fear,'" Lachtman answered, but couldn't bring himself to whip out the hat and plunk it on his head. Throughout the rest of the next hour of the meeting I caught him reaching into that bag six times. He never did get up enough nerve to touch it, let alone put it on his head. I was tempted to do it for him, like my sister-in-law Ruth plunking a leather aviator's cap on one of my nephews, Nat or Dave.

The preliminaries were painful and unswift. The Pierces had small photographs of London taken in 1937. They were passed around photo by photo while the Pierces alternated in telling how they thought each photo showed some location from a Holmes story.

The next order of business was the mysterious Campbell report. Lachtman gave the floor over to Richard Campbell, who turned out to be the man with the cape. He rose with a flourish, threw back his cape, stroked his thin moustache, and strode to the front table past a beagle-faced waiter, who had already started to clear off plates. Campbell gave the waiter a deadly glare, which did no good, and spoke.

"My report," he began, the time between the two words equaling the duration of the Battle of Midway, "is not fully prepared. But it soon will be. Mark my word. It soon will be."

With that he returned to his seat and folded his arms, waiting for someone to dare criticize him.

"Cynthia Brewer," mumbled Aardvark.

The superior sneer left Campbell's face. His eyes darted back and forth as if reading frantically through his memory of all the tales of Conan Doyle in a mad frenzy to recover the forgotten name.

"Challenge," he shouted at Aardvark, who didn't look up.

"He challenged," I said to Randisi, whose eyes were cast forlornly on the disappearing sherbet.

"What?" said Aardvark, brushing a wisp of orange hair from his forehead.

"He challenged Cynthia Brewer," came a voice, an old lady voice.

Aardvark's confusion was evident.

"He challenged Cynthia Brewer?"

"He did," I said. "Who is she?"

"She's a sophomore in my early American history class," he said. "How does he know her? I was just thinking . . ."

"And now," said Lachtman the meek and bald, rising with a prod from Officer Margaritte before he could make another swipe at the deerstalker challenging him in his shopping bag, "Lou will introduce our speaker for the night."

He sat down and all eyes turned to Randisi, whose head was down completely, lost in the scotch memory of Cynthia Brewer.

We waited for several months for Randisi to stir, but the best he could do was reach up and remove his name card. We all watched in fascination as he turned it right-side up, considered putting it back on, and let it fall to the table. I introduced myself.

"What part," asked an ancient woman with incongruously blond hair, "does deduction play in your solving cases?"

"Almost none," I said.

"Then how do you help your clients, catch criminals, restore order?" demanded Campbell.

"I'm stubborn," I said, looking around the room for my suspect. "I take whatever passes for a lead, and I keep after it. Sometimes I go after ten leads before I get anywhere, and sometimes I go after twenty leads and never get anywhere. My trick is to never give up."

"Do the police ever seek your help on baffling cases?" came another female question.

The question had a sting to it. She was thinking Holmes. I was thinking that my being in this very room was the result of the only time in my life that a cop had asked me for help. I skipped that exception and gave the rule: that cops thought I was a pest, which I was, that they caught far more con men, thieves, and killers than I did and did it a lot more efficiently.

More questions came, and I kept giving answers, but not the ones they wanted to hear. The only one that seemed to please them was that I liked my work.

When I sat down Lachtman got up, thanked me, and everyone clapped politely. The meeting ended with Lachtman asking for suggestions about the next meeting. One little old lady, filled with enthusiasm, said aloud, "I've got it. Let's put on a play."

While this never failed to get a rise from Judy Garland when Mickey Rooney said it, no one in the group even gave an indication that the woman had spoken.

Campbell rapped his cane on the table and stood.

"I suggest that when next we meet, we have a Sherlockian quiz prepared by our current president and that the winner of that quiz have his dinner paid for."

"Or her dinner," came a powerful rasp.

"As the case may be," conceded Campbell, sitting with a smirk that indicated clearly who he expected to win the quiz.

"Sounds like a fine idea," agreed Lachtman, looking around for support. Margaritte turned her head away. Meanwhile, Aardvark's head was sinking dangerously close to the pool of melted sherbet. I nudged him, and he roused himself into something that resembled being awake.

"Settled," said Lachtman. "I'll prepare the quiz. And that's it for tonight. I'm glad you could all—"

Campbell was already up and had turned his back to address a group at another table before Lachtman could finish his goodbye.

With the possible exception of Campbell, who didn't seem to be a particularly good suspect, no one in the room really resembled the one who had tried to kill me two days earlier at Mae West's party, but then again it was hard to know. The person might well be a woman, though there were some reasons to think it wasn't.

With the opportunity for the deerstalker gone till the next meeting, Lachtman turned to me.

"Thank you for coming to speak to us tonight, Mr. Pastor. We've all learned a great deal about how a detective works."

His words and the response of the group had made it clear that they really didn't care how a real detective worked and that I had, as many times before in my battered life, disappointed people who expected more from me.

Margaritte Lachtman moved to her husband's side as the crowd aimed for the door.

"It was fun," I lied. "Was this the entire group or were there some members who couldn't make it?"

"Everyone was here," Lachtman said, looking at his wife for confirmation. She didn't confirm.

"Ressner," she corrected. "Jeffrey Ressner."

"Yes, oh yes, Mr. Ressner," Lachtman remembered, with a look on his face that reminded me of the time my brother had slipped me a worm at a Saturday matinee when I had asked for the popcorn.

"What about Mr. Ressner?" I said with a small smile.

"He hasn't come in several years, though he called yesterday and said he was back," said Lachtman, looking at the door. "He knows the Canon well and many other things, but—"

"He is a bit difficult, or was in the past," completed Margaritte, handing Lachtman his shopping bag.

"Maybe it's just too far for him to come," I tried.

"He doesn't live that far, no farther than some members, somewhere in the valley with his daughter," he said.

That was as far as I could push. I should be able to find a Jeffrey Ressner in the valley phone books. Of course he might be living with a daughter under her name, and she might have a married name, and Lachtman would surely have an address for him, and I might have to come back and get it, but for now I had a lead.

"It was good to meet you, Mr. Peters," said Margaritte Lachtman, extending her hand. Maybe it was one Pepsi too many and an overload of caloric energy, but her hand felt like Anne's and I didn't want to let it go. She pulled away and moved toward Alvin Aardvark, who had passed out at the main table. Busboys and waiters were clearing up around him as I moved to leave.

In the next room the salesmen masquerading as politicians were laughing, probably at the jokes of their boss. I didn't laugh when Campbell swooped in front of me as I took a step into the hall.

"You were asking about Jeffrey Ressner," he said.

I shrugged. "Not particularly."

"You were asking," he insisted, pointing his cane at me. I considered taking it from him and playing a few Krupa tunes on his head. "I suggest you stay away from him. He is more dangerous than Lethal and Lightning."

"Lethal and Lightning?"

"Yesterday at San Quentin," he said softly between the peals of next-door laughter, "Robert S. James was hanged. He was a barber convicted of killing pregnant Mary Bush James, his wife, for twenty-one thousand dollars insurance. He drowned her after failing to kill her by forcing her to put her feet into a box that contained two rented rattlesnakes named Lethal and Lightning. A tale worthy of the master himself."

"I'll keep it in mind," I said.

With that Campbell made a move intended, I think, to give the impression that he had disappeared into the shadows behind a potted palm. Instead, he tripped over the scurrying, chunky little beagle of a waiter and fell with his cane clattering and his hand grabbing for fronds.

"Drunken fart," mumbled the waiter, hurrying on.

I tried to pretend that I hadn't seen Campbell's failed exit and headed for the door and home.

CHAPTER 3

Dinah Shore sang "One Dozen Roses" to me as I drove to my office in the Farraday Building the next morning. I took Melrose to Vermont and cut across at Ninth. The news tried to come on and tell me about the Russian front and to remind me that they were going to draft 1Bs, but I wouldn't listen. I turned the radio off as I pulled into the alley off Hoover, where I usually parked between garbage cans and piles of soggy newspapers. The newspapers were gone. Kids had grabbed them up on red wagons and carted them off to school paper drives.

There were no downtown bums sleeping it off at the back door, and the world inside the dark coolness of the Farraday Building was (as I always remembered it) filled with the smell of Lysol, faint echoes, and the distant clicking of machines including typewriters, the mildly porno press on the third floor, and an out-of-tune piano.

My back, which would have qualified me as 4F even if I weren't too old and didn't have too many dents in my cranium and the red kiss of two bullet wounds in my gut, was giving me warnings. Soaking in rain and a cold pool had done me no good. So I moved slowly and quietly. Somewhere in the depths of cracked marble and pebble glass office windows Jeremy Butler lurked, cleaning and rhyming. If he spotted me moving slowly, he'd insist on working on my back. His manipulations always gave me relief, but the immediate pain of his knee in my back and his hairy arms around my chest was sought only in the most extreme emergencies. I had no emergency.

My plan, as I walked the wide fake marble stairs upward toward the fourth floor, was to track down Ressner or whoever the extortionist was and turn him over to the cops before he went for Mae West again or made a move at me for messing up his scam. I hadn't liked the cracked voice behind all that makeup and I didn't look forward to opening my front door one day and finding Ressner disguised as Rita Hayworth with a gun in his hand.

On the second floor I paused to give my back a rest and heard the echo of footsteps below and the opening of the elevator door. It was a newcomer to the Farraday Building. Only newcomers or the terminally ill rode the elevator, an ornate brass cage that gave the illusion it wasn't moving at all, that the building was slowly sinking around it. Usually it stalled by the second floor, and the rider had to force the metal door open and walk the rest of the way. Bad back and all, I was sure I'd beat the elevator to four, if it was going that far, with enough time to spare for a cup of Shelly Minck's caramel thick coffee.

Somewhere in the deck of offices on two, a groan rattled the glass of an unseen door. My guess was that it came from the offices of the Bookends of Jesus, a recent Farraday tenant run by twin grinners with white hair and Iowa accents. Jeremy had said that they had nothing in their office but heavy cartons and a telephone, which made them among the more stable occupants of the Farraday.

My favorite tenant, however, was Alice Palice, who in the farthest corner of the third floor ran Artistic Books, an economical operation consisting of one small porno printing press weighing 250 pounds, considerably less than Alice, who frequently had to hoist the machine on her shoulder and run like hell when a complaint came. I think Alice had designs on Jeremy, the only creature in greater Los Angeles who could lift both Alice and her nonportable press.

When I hit four, the elevator was far below and making a familiar weary metal sound.

Bookies, alcoholic doctors, baby photographers with thick glasses, and con artists on the way down paced and called behind their glass cages as I went up one more flight in the Farraday. In the building across the street the same thing was happening. I imagined a world of multiplied Farraday Buildings teaming with mildew and the last gasp of false energy. I wondered how many of the people in these buildings were 1Bs. Maybe the Bookends of Jesus were both 1Bs and could be stuffed flatfooted and nearsighted into uniforms and shipped off to General MacArthur to plug a leak in the Pacific.

In front of my office door I paused and read the familiar sign in black letters on the pebbled glass:

SHELDON P. MINCK, D.D.S.,S.D.
DENTIST

If you looked, you could see through the swatch of white paint that the words *Oral Surgeon* had been covered over. Shelly had reluctantly blotted them out after a visit from a not-very-friendly representative of the dental association.

In much smaller letters below this was:

TOBY PETERS

PRIVATE INVESTIGATOR

I went in. The small reception room was as it always had been: three wooden chairs, small table with an overflowing ashtray, copies of magazines going back to the Jazz Age, and a dusty pharmaceutical house drawing of a tooth. I went through the room to Shelly's dental office, where he was singing "Bye Bye Blackbird" as he worked on a kid in uniform. The kid was sitting at attention.

"Be with you in a min-oot," bellowed Shelly, waving a bloody swab in my general direction.

"It's me," I said, stepping up to look at the kid, whose eyes were glistening with tears of pain he just barely controlled. He was, I guessed, about ten years old. Almost all soldiers, sailors, and marines looked as if they were ten years old, but with 1Bs being called up, maybe that would change. The armed forces would look like a convention of pops and sons, hand in hand, skipping up on the Nazis and Japs.

"Toby," Shelly said, turning to me to squint through his ever-sagging thick glasses. He removed his cigar from his mouth, which let me think he had something serious to say, wiped the bloody swab on his once-white smock, and went on. "Been waiting for you."

"Thanks," I said, heading for the coffeepot. There was enough in it for one last cup. I poured it into an almost-clean brown cup and waited. Log Cabin syrup in the little metal cabin poured faster.

"Working on this boy for practically nothing," Shelly said proudly, rubbing his sweaty bald head with his sleeve. "Mean breaks on the bicuspids." Shelly reached for the kid's mouth, and the kid shrank back, but there was no place to go. "Got in a fight. You know? Big night in the big city."

"I thought the army had its own dentists," I said, trying to remove my sugar spoon from the coffee.

"They do, they do," Shelly agreed, putting a plump and not-too-clean hand on the boy's shoulder, "But Private Bayer here didn't want to get into any trouble." Shelly shot us both a wink of dark conspiracy. "And I'm only too happy to help our boys in blue."

"He's a soldier, not a sailor," I said, chewing on a mouthful of coffee. I put the cup down in the sink, which was already filled with used dental tools and a plate smeared with something red, probably Shelly's strawberry breakfast roll.

The kid tried to swallow and smile back at Shelly, who looked down at him benevolently.

"If that's his pleasure," I said, looking at the kid.

"Sure it is," grinned Shelly, searching for something in the stack of instruments on the little table. The kid's eyes opened wide and carried the prayer that whatever Shelly came up with it wouldn't be sharp and more than six inches long. Shelly didn't find what he wanted, so he moved next to me and looked in the sink. Below a stainless-steel pan with egg stains on it he found what he was searching for. It was sharp, or had been once, and maybe less than six inches long. The kid groaned. Shelly washed the instrument under the cold water and leaned toward me, smelling of stale cigar and mint Life Savers.

"Client," he whispered.

"You mean someone called?" I whispered back.

The kid in the chair leaned forward, straining to hear us. Maybe we were consulting on his case, life, and future.

"No," whispered Shelly coming even closer. "In your office, now. Clean suit. Been waiting almost an hour. Guy was here when I opened up."

I took off my hat, clenched my fist at the kid to encourage him, and took the three steps to my office as Shelly went back to the work with the weapon in hand.

Clients almost never came to my office. I discouraged it. When someone called, I usually went to him or her or arranged to meet at the drugstore at the corner or Manny's taco stand on Flower Street, depending on how high-class the potential client was. This guy was a little hard to place. He looked up at me from the papers on his lap as I closed the door.

"Peters," I said.

He put the papers into his briefcase, stood, and held out his hand. I took it. His shake was firm and his eyes on mine.

"Winning, Dr. Robert Winning," he said. Winning was about five ten, average build, and well but conservatively dressed in a dark suit, white shirt, and dark blue tie with thin angular stripes of a slightly lighter blue. The lighter blue matched his eyes. I guessed he was somewhere in his fifties. His hair was dark brown without a touch of gray, and his skin had that smooth clearness that comes with heredity or illness. He sat straight and watched as

I moved behind my desk, unbuttoned my own blue jacket carefully to keep the button that was on its last thread from falling off, and looked at him.

"I'm looking for a man and I want you to help me find him," Winning said. His voice was calm like a radio announcer's. "His name is Jeffrey Ressner."

There are coincidences in the world and there is magic. I believe in both, but only after all other explanations have been exhausted. My eyes must have showed something because Winning smiled.

"I know," he said. "I've been trying to find Ressner for a week. I checked some of his old known contacts and talked this morning to Howard Lachtman, of the Engineer's Thumbs. He told me that you had asked about Ressner, and he gave me your address. I decided that it would be best if I could discover why you are seeking Ressner and to enlist your aid in that effort."

I glanced down at my mail. There were three items. One was a postcard from a clothing store in Van Nuys announcing spring wardrobe suggestions. The second was an official-looking letter with a government return address. It looked like one of the notices to register for ration cards. I threw it in the trash can under my desk. The other mail was a square envelope. I recognized the writing and wanted to open it, but I had business. Instead I picked it up and played with it as I talked.

"Why do you want Ressner?" I asked.

Winning pulled some papers from his briefcase, glanced at them, and looked at me.

"I'm a psychiatrist," he said softly. "Head of the Winning Institute near Clovis, just beyond Fresno. Mr. Ressner, until April fifteenth of this year, was a patient in our institute and had been for more than four years. He escaped dressed rather ingeniously as a nurse."

"What was he in for?" I asked trying not to look at the envelope, which had definitely been addressed by my ex-wife, Anne.

Winning blew out a little puff of air and shook his head. He could either make this long or short, and I had the feeling that he had given the long version before.

"Simply put," he began, "Jeffrey Ressner is obsessed with famous people. He believes that fame was denied him as a young man when he had a promising acting career. In fact, he seems to have been a reasonably competent and perhaps even gifted actor, but as you know, talent is not always enough. He began to harass movie producers, actors, directors, and others for jobs, and the police were called in several times. It grew increasingly worse to the point where his wife and daughter left him. Subsequently, both the wife and daughter showed some understanding and agreed to have him taken in for treatment. Fortunately, Ressner's wife had since remarried someone with considerable financial resources."

"How bad was he?"

"Nothing terrible, really," sighed Winning. "A few situations in which he had to be removed by the police from Cecil B. De Mille's house. One confrontation with Joe Louis."

"Joe Louis? What did he have—"

"That was never made quite clear to us," Winning said, showing a trace of puzzlement. "Ressner said something about Joe Louis as a performer of . . . but it wasn't clear."

"Mae West," I said.

"What?" he gasped.

"Has Ressner ever had any contact with Mae West?" I said.

"You surprised me with that," he said. "Miss West appeared at the institute last year. She is very interested in the problems of the mentally ill, among other things. Ressner met her and tried to talk to her. We had to pull him away. He grew more and more animated, insisting that she could help his career. How did you know . . .?"

"I think he contacted her," I explained, starting to tear the corner off the envelope. "Bad scene at her place night before last, Dr. Winning. I think your Mr. Ressner is dangerous. I think you should call in the cops."

Winning's already pale face grew even more pale.

"No, no. Not if it can be helped. He's never done anything really violent and the embarrassment to the institute, his family, our . . . I'd rather avoid it if at all possible."

"He tried to turn me into diced ham," I said, inserting my finger under the letter flap.

"Mr. Peters," Winning stood, leaning both hands on my desk. It put him above me, looking down, which might have worked on difficult patients or their relatives, but only resulted in my turning a near smirk in his direction. "Our institute does some fine work. One of our new patients, for example, should the family so decide, will be Kermit Roosevelt, Teddy Roosevelt's son. It can do us no good to have the police brought in followed by the newspapers talking about escaped lunatics and . . . you can see my point."

"My fee, Dr. Winning, is thirty bucks a day plus expenses, plus three percent over expenses to cover paperwork. I'll take the case for four days. If I don't have him by then, we take it to the cops. Agreed?"

Winning sat again.

"Perhaps we can discuss it if you haven't found him in four days?"

We were bargaining for pennies.

"Sure," I agreed. "I'll call you at the institute if I haven't got a line on him by Monday, but it'll just be to let you know that it's time to go to the cops. Deal?"

Winning touched his chin with his right hand, shrugged, and said, "It is a deal."

"I'll need fifty dollars up front," I said. He pulled out his wallet and fished for the fifty in tens and ones while I glanced at the invitation to my wife's wedding in two days. I dropped Winning's card on the desk on top of Nelson Rockefeller's face on the cover of *Life*.

I took the bills from Winning, stuffed them in my wallet, and pulled a pad of paper out of my top drawer. The top sheet had my doodle of cubes attached to cubes. I ripped it off, wrote a receipt, handed the sheet to him, and he fished out and handed me a business card, white, clean, embossed in silver, in hard-to-read script.

"Call me at any time of the day or night," he said, rising and snapping his briefcase closed. "If my secretary or I do not answer, please keep trying. The institute is a rather busy place, and I spend little actual time in my office."

I looked down at my invitation to a wedding and then at the psychiatrist.

"You married, doc?"

"I was," he said, looking at me as if I might be a suitable case for treatment. "My duties proved to take more time and attention than my wife could accept."

"I know how it is," I said. "My wife's getting remarried in two days."

"Would you like to give me the fifty dollars back and talk about it for a few hours," he said with a smile.

"No, I think I'll hold on to the cash and try to work it out myself. Is that what you guys get? Twenty-five bucks an hour?"

"You can get less expensive help," he said, "but it's not always as good."

"Forget it. You have any information on Ressner I might be able to use? A photo?" I said, unable to look up from the invitation.

"Right on your desk, in that folder, but no photo," Winning said softly.

I hadn't noticed him putting the folder there.

"I'll be in touch," I said with a nod and a look toward Winning, who had walked to the door and had his hand on the knob. He was looking beyond my eyes for something deeper, but I had dropped the shades. Winning gave up, opened the door, and let in the sound of Shelly scraping away and singing, "Where nobody cares for me, sugar's sweet, so is she." Then he was gone, and I was alone with my invitation and last week's *Life*.

I read the thin file Winning had dropped on my desk. Winning had been a sweet break. I was going for Ressner anyway, for myself, for Mae West, and for Phil. Getting paid for it would be nice.

There was no likely Ressner in the L.A. directory. Same was true of the valley towns. Nothing in the files helped much except for a reference to Ressner's former wife. Her name was now Grayson. Which reminded me—Anne Mitzenmacher Peters would soon be Anne Howard.

I couldn't find a Jeanette Grayson in any of the directories, but that didn't surprise me much. The phone, if it was listed, would be in her husband's name, and there were too damn many Graysons to start that. The file had no address or phone number for her. So, I looked up at my favorite crack in the white wall of my office, followed it to the corner, and picked up the phone.

Phil wasn't in, but his partner, Sergeant Steve Seidman, a silent cadaver of a man, asked if he could help. I said no and told him to have Phil call back. Then I waited.

At first I searched for letters to write. There weren't any. I doodled cubes and tried to find a position on the chair that didn't make my back worse. Then I looked out the window at the alley and watched a pair of rummies heading toward the Farraday. I lost sight of them below. I would have forgotten them if I didn't hear something like metal against concrete. I pried open the window and leaned out to see the two bums prying off my hubcaps.

My .38 was in the glove compartment. Even if I had it, I wouldn't have fired even a warning shot. I don't shoot well enough. I'd probably kill one of them, put another hole in my car, or fill an innocent passerby with dread and lead. I grabbed a bronze paperweight shaped like Alcatraz and shouted down.

"Drop those caps and run like hell," I yelled. "Or I'll bomb you clear to Burbank."

"Drop them," I shouted, "or . . ."

I heaved Alcatraz out the window and watched it turn over three or four times before hitting the roof of my car, bouncing and crashing through the rear window. The bums, thinking that they were being bombed by God, dropped the caps and ran. One cap spun like a top. The other rolled back toward the car and leaned against it.

That's when the phone rang.

"You think you've got troubles," I said to whoever was on the other end.

"Can the crap, Tobias," came Phil's weary voice. "What do you want?"

"Help," I said.

He didn't answer.

"With the job we talked about," I went on.

"What do you need?" he said quietly.

"I've got to find a woman in the Los Angeles area named Grayson, first name Jeanette. I think she's married to someone with money. Her ex-husband is probably the looney who went after Mae West."

"You at your office?" he said.

"Yeah, I'm at my office. Anne's getting married Sunday."

He didn't say anything, just breathed heavy.

"Sunday," I repeated.

"What do you want me to say?" he finally sighed. "She knows what she's doing. It's your own fault. You've heard it all. Get off the phone and let me see if I can get this for you."

He hung up. I needed someone to feel sorry for me, so I wandered into Shelly's office where he was humming "The Carioca" and patting the mouth of the soldier with a gray towel as if he were a baby who had dribbled a mouthful of banana mush.

"Don't bite on that for a week or two," Shelly paused in his humming to say.

The kid nodded and looked at the door.

"That filling and stuff will hold all right," Shelly went on as he chomped on his cigar, "but it's not made to be abused. You're going to have to be careful chewing on that side from now on. Your new life motto is 'Eat Carefully and Chew on the Right.'"

The kid nodded again, got up, dug out a wallet, and counted out bills, which he handed to Shelly, who removed his cigar. Shelly always removed his cigar to count money. Satisfied, he beamed at the kid, who beat it into the dangerous halls of the Farraday Building.

"Shel," I said softly. "Anne's getting married Sunday."

Shelly looked at me and blinked behind his bottle-bottom glasses.

"Too bad," he said shaking his head. "Say, did you have any money down with Arnie on the Sugar Ray Robinson fight? Knocked out Banner in the second. I made twenty bucks."

"Anne's getting married," I repeated as he stuffed the money into his wallet.

"Anne?"

"My former wife," I explained.

"That airlines guy you were talking about? Ralph?" he said, pushing his glasses back and reaching for a dental journal.

"That's the one," I admitted.

Shelly sat in his own chair, magazine in his lap, and looked at me with sympathy.

"Mildred and I want to visit her brother in Cleveland," he said. "You think Anne could get this guy to give us a break on tickets?"

"I'll ask him, Shel. Thanks for listening."

"What are friends for," he said with a knowing smile and settled down with his journal.

The phone call came an hour later. I had spent the hour trying to think about something else. A client once tried to teach me meditation as payment for finding his runaway sister. I got the idea down all right, but I couldn't put it into practice. My thoughts, my back, the damn city, and my dreams kicked me in my flat nose every time I tried. The guy had assured me that if I just kept at it I'd make a breakthrough one day. I had almost given up on that ever happening, but I gave it a try every so often. The problem was that I had chosen the bronze Alcatraz paperweight as the focus of my attention during meditation and it was resting somewhere inside my Buick.

"Forty-six Buena Suerte in Plaza Del Lago," came Phil's voice over the phone.

"Got it," I said.

"You going to the wedding?"

"Sure," I said. "Wouldn't miss it for a dozen tacos and all the Pepsi in Ventura."

CHAPTER 4

The Graysons had a phone, but there was no answer. It took me five minutes to find Plaza Del Lago on the Mobil Oil map I kept in my bottom drawer. After two more minutes I decided that the map was just too old, that Plaza Del Lago was one of the hundreds of new towns that had sprung up in the last decade, a period my map didn't cover.

I found it at about the point where I was going to give up, climb in my Buick, and make what would probably be my final fruitless attempt to pull a teardrop of affection from Anne. Plaza Del Lago wasn't on the coast where I had been looking. It was inland, beyond Palmdale, almost touching the Mojave Desert, maybe sixty miles from Hollywood off of State Highway 138.

Shelly was absorbed in his dental journal when I walked out. I don't think he heard me say that I'd be gone till Monday. It didn't matter; I wasn't expecting any calls.

The damage to the Buick wasn't too bad: a dent in the roof that cut through four or five layers of paint and a broken window. I fished out fragments of glass, placed Alcatraz gently on the front seat, and drove to No-Neck Arnie's. He was working on a recent Caddy.

"Arn, this is an emergency," I said, getting out.

He sighed, the sigh of the put-upon mechanic, a sigh that Alexander the Great probably got from his blacksmith when he came in with a battle-battered chariot.

"I see," he said, touching the dent. "Bombed by an eagle with kidney stones."

"No," I answered. "Alcatraz fell from the sky."

Arnie didn't care whether I was joking or not. He fixed cars, took a few bets on the side, and went through life without a sense of humor, which is probably located somewhere in the neck.

"Forget about the dent," he said. "Live with it. There's a war on. This car ain't going to make it through it. I'll fix the window or give it a patch, some clear, thick see-through stuff. If I fix the window, it stays here two, three days. I can put the patch on in five minutes for five bucks. You want my advice?"

"No," I said. Five bucks was a hell of a lot for some tape and see-through stuff.

He decided to give me the advice anyway, but he looked around to be sure no one was listening. To do this, Arnie had to turn his entire tub of a body.

"Let me junk the parts on this carroodi and you can subtract it from the cost of that '38 Ford we were talking about the other day. It would only run you two hundred and twenty bucks."

"The other day you said I could have the Ford for two hundred with no junk parts. No questions." I reminded him.

"There have been other bidders," he confided, looking down at his grease-black hands and rubbing the tips of his fingers together.

"I'll keep the carroodi for a few days and think about it," I said. "Meanwhile, try to keep the price on that Ford from hitting three hundred."

"I'll try," he said laying a hand on my shoulder and doing something with his mouth that resembled a smile.

I had never considered Arnie a friend, and he wasn't bringing us any closer together, but I could give lopsided smiles with the best of them. We could have stood there grinning like baboons in Griffith Park for an hour or so, but I had no time for such jollity.

"Put the stuff on the back window, and here's five before the price goes up."

Ten minutes later I was on my way to Plaza Del Lago after Arnie told me that I still had time to put a few bucks on the Kentucky Derby, which was scheduled to start in an hour.

"Put two bucks on Shutout," he confided, leaning into my window.

"Next year," I said, glancing back through the blue thickness of my double-layered rear window.

I drove for an hour, listening to the radio. A big battle was going on at the gates of Mandalay. I tried not singing "The Road to Mandalay," but it came out anyway. The sports news came on around one and I was told that Willard Marshall was expected to be a big gun for Mel Ott's Giants. I remembered seeing Ott a couple of times in exhibition games, that bottle of a bat and that foot up in the air when he moved into the ball. Next weekend I'd get my nephews Dave and Nat and take them to a ball game somewhere, if my sister-in-law Ruth would let me. She didn't really trust me with them since the last time I had taken the boys out, promising to take them to see *Dumbo*, and dropping them instead at a triple horror show that gave Davie nightmares for a week. When the announcer told me that Shutout had won the Derby, I turned the radio off.

The land went flat about two minutes past Dot's Dixie Gas Station, just inside Antelope Valley, where I had stopped to fill the tank and buy a candy bar.

Antelope Valley was named for the herds that roamed there a few hundred years earlier at the edge of the Mojave. Low hills, the Lovejoy Buttes, separate the valley from the desert. The twenty-five-hundred-square-mile valley is supplied with water from a giant natural reservoir underground and runoff from the mountains.

In April and May tourists from town come out to see the desert flowers, particularly the California poppies that sometimes stretch like a red blanket for twenty miles. I had gone slowly behind tourists for much of the way.

Dot was a skinny guy with a bad leg and no interest in conversation. A mongrel dog, which was stuffed, dead, or in deep meditation, lay next to the pump where Dot filled me up after looking at the dent in my roof and the rear window.

The flat land turned to desert brush and stretched on dry and far past Palmdale. I was somewhere near Plaza Del Lago or what once had been Plaza Del Lago, but it wasn't there. Then the narrow road took a sudden dip, and I saw the town sitting in a basin. It was bigger than I expected and sprawled out. A narrow part of town lay in front of me on both sides of the two-lane highway with wooden storefronts and old houses. Beyond the street on both sides stood larger, more substantial houses with grounds and an occasional pool. Face-to-face off the highway, about a block in to the left, were two big sprawling buildings both with large pools.

Five minutes later I was on Plaza Del Lago's main street and pulling into a parking space in front of Cal's General Store and Gifts. I went in, plunked down a quarter and got a box of Wheaties and a quart of milk and two cents in change from a woman I supposed was Mrs. Cal, a thin-haired knot of a woman dressed in overalls. I'd worry about a bowl and spoon later.

"Could you tell me where the Grayson place is?" I said, hoisting my bag of groceries.

"Could," said Mrs. Cal and turned back to stacking Gold Dust Cleanser.

"Will you?" I went on.

She looked at me in a way that would have put Arnie's sigh to shame.

"You got business?" she said. Her voice had a desert dry rattle, resulting I imagined from eating nothing but crackers from the cracker barrel and conserving her voice for the opera.

"I got business," I said, getting into the swing of things.

"They're new, practically everyone is here," she said, looking at me in a way that made it clear that I would not be a welcome addition to Plaza Del Lago.

"Why'd they all come?"

"The springs," she said, pointing at a display across the aisle behind me. The store wasn't big, and the two aisles were narrow and filled from floor to ceiling. The display she pointed to was bottles of something called Poodle Springs water. The labels were yellow with a white cartoon poodle on them, standing on its hind legs, with its tongue out. The water inside the bottle was a little murky.

"Spring under the town," Mrs. Cal explained, growing talkative. "Been there since God created it."

"That a fact?" I encouraged.

"Stuff tastes like turkey piss," she said, shaking her head.

Never having tasted turkey piss I said, "No kidding."

"I don't kid," she said, leaning on the counter.

"How'd it all start?"

"Fella named Grayson, the one you're looking for, come down here maybe ten years back, bought up most of the land. People were happy to sell it to him. Thought he was a idiot."

"He wasn't?" I asked.

"Look around if you got eyes," she said, turning her head in every direction. All I could see was piles of groceries, but I assumed she meant the buildings beyond. "He got all kinds of fools from places like San Francisco, Los Angeles, and Reno to put up money and build houses and those two hotels. Sunk money into ads in the papers. Told people this turkey piss could cure anything. Pretty soon old people were down here buying, swimming in the stuff, drinking it. Some people will buy a goat's ass and stick it on their head if a smart talker gets his jaw going at them."

"Some people," I agreed.

"We make out all right with it," she added. "I ain't complaining."

Since it had sounded to me like complaining, I considered debating the point with her, but remembered my job.

"Grayson's?"

"Keep going two roads east, turn left and drive till you can't drive no more. Big 'dobe house with an old mission bell on top and a Joshua tree in the yard."

"Thanks," I said, taking my package and turning.

Mrs. Cal went back to her stacking and piling without another word.

The directions were fine. Plaza Del Lago wasn't that big. I passed the two face-to-face hotels with porches covered with old people wearing floppy hats and drinking murky turkey piss. None of them had a goat's ass on their head, unless it was under the floppy hats.

The fronts of the houses further down were landscaped with sand, rocks, and cactus. Poles with telephone and electric lines hovered over the houses and connected them down the road.

At the end of the road touching the desert was a yellow adobe house with a mission bell on the roof and a Joshua in the yard. I parked at the rough wooden gate and went up the sandy path. The Joshua was in bloom.

The Joshua isn't a real tree, just a California imitation, a kind of yucca, named by early Mormon settlers, who remembered the book of Joshua: "Thou shalt follow the way pointing for thee by the tree."

The Joshua starts out life branchless, standing like a pole on the desert, then starts putting out clumsy limbs pointing out and up with green bristles on the end like bayonets. The leaves die, turn gray-brown and lie back along the branches giving the plant a weird shaggy outline. Blossoms appear on the end of each branch from March to June, clusters of waxy cream white flowers, They smell like mushrooms.

My old man, when he had a spare afternoon, used to like to drive out and look at the Joshua trees. He remembered the time the London *Daily Telegraph* had sent out crews of Chinese to cut down trees ot make paper pulp. But, he said, God had intervened, spoiled the first shipment back to England, and a terrible rainstorm had routed the Chinese cutting crew.

I moved on to the front door shaded by a small porch. On either side of the door were wooden lounge chairs so that Grayson could sit in the evening and watch his town go to sleep.

I knocked and knocked again—nothing but a faint sound inside the house that might have been someone moving around or could have been the normal aches and groans of a late afternoon. I walked around to the side of the house, loosening my jacket, and popped the button that had been threatening to depart for a month. I knelt to retrieve it among the stones and sand and felt a shadow over me.

"What are you doing?"

The voice was a woman's. The age was unclear. I squinted up into the sun and saw her outline. She seemed to be naked.

"I lost my button," I said, spotting it and stuffing it into my pocket. I got up and could see that she wasn't naked but wearing a white bathing suit.

"I meant, what are you doing here, sneaking around our house?"

"Mrs. Grayson?" I said, stepping to the side to get a look at her.

"Miss Ressner," she said. "Delores Ressner. What are you doing here?"

She was tall, maybe even taller than I, with a good, trim figure, short brown hair, and blue eyes. She seemed to be about thirty.

"I want to talk to your mother," I said, trying not to finger the threads on my jacket, which had just given up their responsibility for holding that button. I was sweating and uncomfortable. She was tall and demanding.

"What about?" she said without moving.

"Your father."

"Harold Grayson isn't my father," she said flatly.

"I know. It's Jeffrey Ressner I want to talk about."

Something fell in her face and facade. A shudder or shiver ran through her tan body. She turned and walked slowly to the back of the house. I followed her. The swimming pool there was small and filled with blue water, not the product from the local spring.

Delores Ressner picked up a towel from a lounge chair near the pool and began to dry herself, giving her time to think, which was all right with me. I had no place to go, and I didn't mind looking at her. When she was through toweling, she slipped into a blue robe. Finished, she turned toward me, folded her arms, and asked: "What do you want to know about my father?"

"I want to know where he is."

"Who are you?" Her eyes had narrowed, and she shook her hair to rid it of a few remaining drops of water or to let it hang loose. It was a nice gesture.

"I'm a private detective. Name's Toby Peters. I've been hired by Dr. Winning of the Winning Institute to find your father. He broke out of the institute four days ago."

"And Dr. Winning thinks he might come here?" Her hands tightened and turned white as they clutched her arms. I couldn't tell if there was an undercurrent of fear or disbelief in her voice.

"No," I said, looking at the house for signs of life before turning back to her. "It's a place to start. Dr. Winning doesn't want him hurt and doesn't want him to hurt anybody."

"My father never hurt anybody," she fired back.

"Maybe," I said. "I think we met the other night, and he expressed something more than verbal hostility."

"I never wanted him in that place," she said. "That was my mother and her husband's idea."

"Maybe I could talk to your mother and . . ." I said, taking a step toward the house.

She unfolded her hands and stepped in front of me.

"My mother isn't here. She went to San Diego to visit her sister. My stepfather is in the house sleeping. He hasn't been feeling well and doesn't want to be disturbed."

We stared at each for two or three minutes, waiting for a break. She didn't give me one, so I tried, "I've got a warm carton of milk and some Wheaties in my car. Maybe we can share a bowl and watch the sun go down while we wait for stepdaddy to wake up."

She couldn't stop the corners of her mouth from curling up from her full lips in a near smile, so I went on.

"I could sew on my button while we laugh at my clothes and you show me the family album. I'd like to see a picture of your father."

She thawed a little and let her palms up.

"There are no decent photographs of my father. There used to be when he was acting, but when he grew . . . when he began to have problems, he tore them all up and refused to have another one taken. We've got one of him dressed as King Lear, but you can't really recognize him in it."

"He played Lear?" I said, taking another step toward the house.

"No." Her head bent and shook sadly. "He dressed as Lear but never played him. Knew the part. I remember when I was a little girl he did scenes for me in our kitchen back in Ventura. He was really good."

"So I've heard," I said. "Can I put my milk in your refrigerator?"

Her head came up cocked to one side quizzically.

"O.K., but let's keep it quiet. Harold can be a bit difficult, especially when he's disturbed during his nap or when my father's name comes up."

She led the way in through the back door. The kitchen was large, pine, and modern with shining steel and a double sink. The refrigerator in the corner made self-satisfied gurgling sounds, and we sat at a kitchen table made of redwood. My milk could wait. I'd drink it on the way back to L.A. Through the side window on the opposite side of the house I could see a big blue car, probably a Packard.

Delores Ressner was tight and edgy as she turned the coffeepot on and sat. She scratched at a bothersome cuticle and bit her lower lip before looking up at me.

"What do you do?" I said. "Besides swimming."

She shrugged. "Some acting. Nothing much. A few small parts at Twentieth Century-Fox. I was in *Blood and Sand*. One of the ladies-in-waiting. Things like that. A little modeling, mostly for mail-order catalogs. Now"—she looked out the window—"Now I'm resting before I go back into the jungle."

"Have you heard from your father in the last four days?"

She looked down at a knot in the wooden table. Behind us the coffeepot bubbled.

Somewhere deeper in the house the floor creaked. It wasn't the creak of weather and sundown, but the creak of a human moving.

"He needs help," she said. "Not the kind of help Dr. Winning gives, imprisoning him. My stepfather, if you want the simple truth, pays to keep my father locked up and out of the way. My mother goes along with it because she can't bear the idea of facing my father again. It wasn't easy for her."

"Or you either," I said.

Her eyes were a little moist.

"I think I hear Grayson getting up," I said.

She touched her cheek nervously and stood.

"Let's have coffee. He can find us here."

"Your father," I repeated, turning toward her. "You've heard from him. I don't want to hurt him. I just want to keep him from hurting you and your mother, other people, maybe even himself."

"Maybe even you?" she said, turning to me from the stove with the coffeepot in her hand.

"Maybe. And maybe I'm doing it for my fee and for a friend. But maybe or no maybes, your old man will be a lot better off if I find him before he gets in more trouble. Delores, believe me, he is in trouble, but not in it so far that he can't be eased out of it with some help from you and me."

It was warm in the kitchen, but Delores pulled her robe across her chest with her free hand and shivered as she stepped forward to pour me a cup and one for herself. Then she sat down again, placing the pot on a wooden trivet. She was working herself up to say something, and I wanted to give her room.

I poured a few spoons of sugar in my cup, put my open palm over the cup to feel the moist warmth, and took a sip.

"He's here," she said softly, so softly that I didn't hear it the first time, or maybe I didn't believe what I heard.

"What?" I said, leaning forward.

"Here. He's here in the other room. In the living room. We were waiting for my mother to come back to decide what we'd do. Harold's not sick or napping. He and my father are trying to work things out, see what . . ."

I got up slowly, very slowly.

"I think I'll just go in and join the conversation," I said gently. "No trouble. Why don't you just sit there and finish your coffee. I'll introduce myself to Grayson. Your father and I have already met, I believe."

She nodded in resigned agreement, her shoulders slumping down as if she had done a day of hard labor.

I walked to the doorway leading into the house from the kitchen and considered taking off my shoes to keep from making noise, but every time I have removed my shoes on a case things have got worse instead of better. I moved on. There were no voices ahead of me, but something was creaking. The hallway I found myself in carried on the lacquered dark wood motif. A print on the wall showed the driving of the golden spike. Leland Stanford glared down on me and the future of the West. To my right I found the living room, but no one was in it. There were two sofas, both oversize and masculine brown, a grand piano, and a rocking chair. The rug was an Indian design with a pattern in the center that looked to me like a snarling demon.

Across the hall opposite the living room were three doors, all closed. Still no voices. I tried the first door. It opened and showed me a bedroom, bright and orange, a woman's room, probably Delores's. There was a faint pleasant odor of scented soap or perfume.

The next door was partly open. I stepped in. It was a much larger bedroom than Delores's. In one corner stood a desk. In another a dresser and twin beds beyond which was a view of the town through a big floor-to-ceiling window. The beds were made up with brown Indian spreads. I could see the design clearly on one bed. The other was obscured by the body of the man on top of it.

The man was gray-haired, around sixty, wearing a heavy blue flannel robe and a long knife in his chest. His arms were spread out and his eyes were wide and surprised. Something creaked from the hall, and I grabbed for a portable radio on the dresser. I swung around, ready to clip Jeffrey Ressner with the white Philco, and stopped just short of clobbering Delores, whose mouth went open in fear.

"Back up," I said, putting my free hand out and placing the radio back on the dresser.

"Where is . . ." she began and saw the body on the bed. I put out both hands to catch her if she fell, but kept my eyes on the doorway. Ressner was almost certainly still in the house.

"God," she whispered.

"That's Grayson?" I whispered, pushing her gently out of the room.

Her eyes were still fixed on the body, but she nodded her confirmation. When I had her around the corner into the living room, her eyes met mine and her head shook a dumb no no no no of disbelief.

"Get on the phone and call the local police," I said very quietly. "Can you do that?"

She didn't answer but kept scanning my face for understanding.

"Can you do that? I'm going to find your father and keep him from any other trouble. Now make that call. O.K.?"

She agreed with her eyes and looked around the familiar room, wondering where the phone was.

"He's dead?"

"Dead," I agreed and went for the front door. I was after my .38. Maybe I'd also grab the bronze Alcatraz and my bag of groceries. Ressner was not my run-of-the-dice killer. If he was the same guy I'd tangled with at Mae West's and it looked as if he were, I wasn't sure what it would take to stop him.

Before I could get to my car, the sound of an engine firing up came from behind me. The dark Packard parked at the side of the house came to life and kicked dust and sand as it shot in front of me. I didn't see the driver clearly, but his shape was about what I remembered and expected of Ressner.

I ran around the side of my Buick, climbed in, closed the door, and took off. Ressner took the road I'd come on, the only road, and he really hit the floorboard. He came close to running down an old couple holding floppy hats on with one hand and drinking murky Poodle piss with the other.

At the main road, he turned toward Palmdale on two wheels and took off, wobbling. On the open road, my old Buick couldn't keep up with the Packard, not even close, but I dogged him. If I could stay within a mile or two, he wouldn't be able to stop, and if he hit civilization, driving that fast he'd pick up a surly cop or two. By now Delores, if she had found the phone, had called what passed for police in Plaza Del Lago. I had no idea of what they might do, but I didn't count on their moving quickly. I dogged on, shoving my .38 in my jacket pocket, where it knocked against my hip until I had to take it out and put it on the seat next to me. Ressner was still in sight, going seventy or eighty down the road. My .38 flew up in the air when I hit a rock or a prairie rat and almost took my right eye. I grabbed the gun in midair and put it in my grocery bag.

We were in sight of Dot's Dixie Gas Station when my Buick died a terrible death. It chugged, gurgled, and belched something that sounded like "The hell with it." Metal dropped out of the front of the car and skidded with the undercarriage shooting sparks into the dusk. I lost control. The carton of milk flew out of the bag to see what was happening and exploded against the front windshield, spraying me and ending any chance I had of coming to a reasonable halt. The car barreled off the road and hit something solid.

I flew into the backseat and agreed with the car. We had been through a lot together. The hell with it. I shut my eyes and waited for my dream companion, Koko the Clown, to lead me out of nowhere, but he didn't come.

When my eyes opened, I was looking into the pale face of Dot's mongrel dog, which was neither stuffed nor dead. He had rotten breath, like all dogs.

The room was small and filled with spare auto parts and small animal cages. The cages contained newts, snakes, and a few field mice. There was a small window in the corner, and beyond it was darkness.

"You ain't dead," said Dot, his hands in his pockets looking down at me.

"Thanks," I answered sitting up.

"Car's dead though," he said, handing me a bottle of Pepsi, which was just what I needed. I sat up, sipped it, and wondered what I had broken this time, but nothing hurt very much. In fact, my back felt better than it had before the crash.

I looked at the flannel shirt and torn pants Dot had put on me and said, "Thanks."

"Trade," Dot said, filling a pipe that appeared magically from his fist. "Those duds, the Pepsi, a meal, and a phone call for the wreck."

I gurgled the Pepsi and thought about it.

"You can keep the Wheaties, the gun, and the statue of Alcatraz," he said.

"A deal," I agreed, toasting him with the Pepsi.

The deal completed, Dot lit his pipe, patted the mongrel, who panted appreciatively, and went to the hot plate in the corner, where something was cooking. He came over with a bowl of chili and some Wonder Bread. I spooned down the chili, sopped up what was left with the bread, and downed the last of my Pepsi before trying to stand. I did a pretty good job and found that I was thinking again.

"My suit," I said. "And your phone."

"Suit's in a box by the front door with the gun, Alcatraz, and Wheaties. Suit's not dry. Needs some cleaning, though Thomas licked some of the milk from it when I pulled you out."

"Thanks," I said, going for the phone.

He waved his pipe at me and said, "Used to know Sergeant York, Alvin York back in the last war."

"That a fact?" I said, trying to raise the operator.

"Fact," he said with satisfaction as he took the empty chili bowl away.

Shelly had left the office. No answer. I could have called him at home, but that would have meant the possibility of talking to his wife, Mildred, who, when we were at our best, refused to speak to or about me. I was definitely a bad influence on Shelly. Jeremy owned no car. I could have called Phil, but that would mean driving all the way back to Hollywood with him. I didn't think I could take my brother for that long, and I knew from experience that he couldn't take me.

So I called Mrs. Plaut's Boardinghouse and prayed that Mrs. Plaut would not answer. She did.

"Mrs. Plaut," I shouted. "This is Toby, Toby Peters. Is Mr. Wherthman there. Gunther Wherthman."

"Plaut's Boardinghouse," she said patiently. It was a subject of intense debate at the boardinghouse. Since Mrs. Plaut could hear practically nothing, we wondered why she insisted on answering the phone and, in fact, fought off anyone who tried to take it from her. We also wondered how she heard it ringing. Perhaps it was the vibrations or a sixth sense given only to the ancient and feisty.

"Gunther Wherthman," I shouted, loud enough to wake Thomas, who had dozed off on the cot where I had been lying.

"Mr. Whertham," she gasped. "Why are you calling? I just saw you into your room."

"Oh shit," I sighed softly.

"You needn't blaspheme," retorted Mrs. Plaut. "Even in your native tongue."

Dot looked at me without curiosity, puffed on his pipe, and dreamed of Sergeant York.

"Peters, Peters, Toby PETERS," I shouted. The veins on my forehead ached.

"Mr. Peelers?" she said after a pause.

"Yes," I gasped.

"He is not here and the police are looking for him again," she explained.

"The police . . ."

"I'll let you talk to Mr. Wherthman," she said, and I heard the phone clink against the wall in the hall.

"Used to work in the estuary down near San Luis," Dot told no one in particular as he took his pipe out and looked into the bowl before returning it to the corner of his mouth.

There is no end to the eccentricity of this world, I observed silently waiting for Gunther, who finally came on after a scraping of the chair in the hall on which he always stood to cope with the phone.

"This is Gunther Wherthman here," he said with his usual accent and dignity.

"This is Toby, Gunther. I've had a slight accident."

"Toby, are you all right?"

"I'm O.K. Can you come and get me? I'll tell you where I am. What did Mrs. Plaut mean about the cops looking for me?"

"You are, it seems wanted for interrogation concerning the murder of a Mr. Grayson. I heard through the door. As you know I am not fond of the Los Angeles police." He paused politely and waited for my next question.

"Was my brother one of the cops who came?"

"That is correct," he said.

I gave him directions and spent the next hour and ten minutes playing poker with Dot, who took me for four bucks and informed me that he would use the money to go into town and see Veronica Lake in *This Gun for Hire*.

"She gets kissed by Robert Preston," he said, his eyes glazing over with the look he reserved for Sergeant York and Veronica Lake.

"I'll have to catch it," I said.

When Gunther arrived, I picked up my package, thanked Dot, petted Thomas, and got into the car next to Gunther. Gunther's Olds was equipped with built-up pedals so he could reach them.

"Little fella," said Dot, pointing at Gunther with his pipe.

"I hadn't noticed," I said, and we pulled into the night heading back to L.A.

CHAPTER 5

The next morning I got up early, had some coffee and the Wheaties, and put on my last suit, a brown wool that looked reasonably good if you didn't get too close. Since it was Sunday, I couldn't get my milk-smelling suit cleaned and the button sewed on, and I couldn't contact Arnie to try to make a deal on the '38 Ford before the price went up again. Dot had remembered to take the license plates off the old Buick and drop them in the box with the other goodies.

A call to the Wilshire District Police Station told me that Phil was in and working. Crime doesn't stop on Sunday. In fact, Saturday night is usually enough to make Sunday a cop's daymare.

No backache. No major bruises. I decided to walk the three miles and take in the California sea air, but by the time I hit Fairfax, the rain had started. I ducked into a doorway and looked for a cab. The streets were not quite empty, but Sunday mornings are not carnival time in Los Angeles. Everybody always seems to be someplace else. Too much land too spread out to absorb us all, but the war was helping make up for it by sending thousands in every day. Common sense would have had it the other way. The coast was the most vulnerable part of the States to Japanese attack. The Japanese were warning us every few days that they were coming. Maybe the bombing of Tokyo last week would give them something else to think about, maybe it wouldn't.

What brought people were the jobs. Soldiers, sailors, and marines shipped out from the coast. The fleet was always coming to San Diego. The big money was in the armed forces, and the jobs were where the big money was.

California was having a love affair with men in uniform. They could drink, shout, maim, and abuse, usually one another, and they'd be forgiven like cute three-year-olds. Civilian guilt paved the way until their time ran out and they had to get on those ships and sail to hell island.

The men in uniform who weren't having a great time in L.A. were the cops. By the time I caught a cab and got to the station, the rain was slowing down. A quartet of uniformed cops stood at the top of the stone steps trying to decide if they should go out into the streets, dampen their uniforms and spirits, and look for the bad guys, who were too damned easy to find.

I went in and nodded at the desk sergeant, an old-timer named Coronet, who nodded back. A sailor was sleeping on the wooden bench against the wall.

"Got rolled," said Coronet, nodding at the kid. "Swears it was two guys and Jean Harlow. I told him Harlow's dead. And if she weren't, why would she roll a sailor?"

"Could have been someone who looked like Harlow?" I said.

Coronet shook his shaggy white head wisely and offered me a

stick of Dentyne. I stuck it in my jacket pocket. He unwrapped his and began to chew.

"Naw," he said. "That makeup, the whole ambience is out of touch."

"Ambience?" I repeated.

"Heard it on 'Believe It or Not' last night," Coronet nodded. "Very educational show. You should catch it."

"I will," I said and went up the twenty creaking brown stairs through the often-kicked wooden door at the top and into the squad room. As it always did, the room smelled of food, humanity, and stale smoke.

Business was booming. Fat Sergeant Veldu sat at his desk with one salami hand in the ample hair of a Mexican kid. Veldu was holding the kid's face inches from his own and whispering. The kid looked scared. I couldn't hear what Veldu whispered because there was too much going on.

Two women dressed for a big night out were sitting on a bench in the corner, smoking and talking as if they were waiting for the maître d' to lead them to a seat at the Café La Male. One of the women, a blond, had a black and purple eye. The other woman had a thick bandage over her ear.

The blond laughed and said over the noise, "You should have bit it off."

Next to them a ragbag wino in a long coat was looking through Veldu's wastebasket. Veldu reached back without taking his hand from the Mexican kid or moving his eyes and coshed the ragbag with his free hand. The ragbag sat up.

My least favorite detective in the solar system, John Cawelti, was sipping coffee and playing with a pencil while he listened to someone on the phone, who didn't give him a chance to speak. Cawelti's checked jacket was off, and his shoulder holster rested comfortably over his heart. As always, except for one time when Jeremy Butler had shaken him up, Cawelti's black hair was plastered down and parted in the middle as if he were about to try out for tenor in a barbershop quartet. He looked up and saw me. I smiled at him. It was love at first sight. Then he made the little gesture that cemented our relationship, and I mouthed "Same to you" and winked. He glared for a few seconds more, jabbed his pencil into his desk, and turned away.

Two uniformed cops were standing over a seated guy built like a

Norwegian tanker. He tried to stand but they pushed him back. He paused, blank-faced, tried to stand again, and the cops pushed him down again. Neither side seemed to be enjoying the game. I could see why the cops didn't want him to get to his feet. He was a dead ringer for heavyweight contender Tami Mauriello.

I spotted Seidman in the corner sitting on his desk going through some papers and made my way to him over bums, through bruisers, ladies of last night, cops, and piles of paper.

He didn't bother to look up. He had cops' eyes and knew when I'd stepped into the squad room.

"Usually we have to go out and find you," he said in his dead, even voice, which matched his complexion. "We changing the rules?"

"I'm getting older and mellower, Steve," I said, sitting next to him on the desk and trying to read with him. He put the papers down, folded his arms over his thin chest, and looked at me.

"So am I, Toby," he said. "And I've been up all night. So has Phil. Now if you go into his office and get him riled up and I have to come in and make peace, I may move a little slower than usual. You may not be lucky. Give it a rest. There's a war on."

"Blessed are the peacemakers," I said.

"For they shall inherit the pieces," he replied. "Go on in. Wait. This is a dumb question but I'll ask it for the record. Did you kill that Grayson in Plaza Del Lago?"

"No," I said, plunging my hands in my pockets and dancing out of the way of Veldu and the Mexican kid, who was waltzing toward the private interrogation room in the far corner.

Seidman went back to reading his file, and I knocked on Phil's office door.

"Come in," he said. In I went.

Phil was seated at his desk. His back was turned, and he was scratching his steely-haired head as he had done for the past thirty years. I closed the door and eased into one of the two chairs on the other side of the desk. His office was no bigger than mine back at the Farraday. His window had an even worse view. He admired the brick wall across the way for a few more seconds, scratched his head once more, and turned to me, folding his hands in front of him on the desk. His eyes were red, and gray stubble covered his face. He'd look better in a beard, but cops couldn't have beards.

"O.K., what have you got for me?" he said.

I reached into my pocket, pulled out the bronze Alcatraz, and placed it on the desk in front of him. He looked down at it without unfolding his hands. I looked at it too.

"This is—" he started.

"Alcatraz," I finished. "A present, a paperweight. I used to have it in my office. Got it from an ex-con named Maloney who did time on the Rock. Thought it would look better in here. Maybe you could refer to it when you wanted to sweat a grumpy killer."

Phil's right eye closed slightly trying to assess the joke. He was capable of heaving the thing at me or picking it up, leaping over the desk, and beating me with it.

"Thanks," he said.

It wasn't going to be easy to get a rise out of my brother this day.

"How are Ruth and the kids?" I tried. That usually bothered him.

"Fine. We were supposed to have a picnic today." He looked out the window. Thunder crackled up the coast. "Sunday. What the hell. Did you kill Grayson?"

"No."

Phil scratched his head again and opened the file in front of him. It was my thick file, already fingerprint-stained and frayed at the corners. The basics were there. I'd been in and out of trouble for a dozen years, though no more than other private eyes.

Phil looked up from the file and glanced at our father's watch on my wrist. It said four o'clock. It was getting better all the time, no more than seven hours off.

"O.K.," Phil sighed. "Woman named Delores Grayson says you drove out to Plaza Del Lago yesterday looking for her father. She tried to keep you from seeing him, but you got away from her in her kitchen and went looking for him. She was scared but followed up a few seconds later. She found you in the old man's bedroom. The guy was dead and you were ready to clobber her with a radio. You forced her into the living room, made her sit, and you ran for the door and beat it. How does that sound to you?"

"Like Hansel and Gretel," I said. "Her name isn't Grayson. It's Ressner. I was looking for her father, her real father, Jeffrey Ressner, the guy I think tried to put the hand on our friend Mae West. He was in the house. She tried to keep me from seeing him. When I got to the bedroom, Grayson was already skewered. I told

Delores to call the cops, and I went for Ressner, who pulled out in a Packard, California 1942 license plate thirty-four fifty-seven. I went after him till my car died. Hell, it committed suicide. Delores Ressner is trying to protect her nut father."

"You didn't see Ressner kill Grayson?" Phil said, reaching up to his neck to loosen his tie, but it was already loose and hanging around his shoulders.

"I didn't even see Ressner clearly when he took off in the Packard," I said.

"The Packard belongs to the Graysons," he said. "It's missing. I'll get the state police to talk to Delores. This isn't my case, Toby. It's the state police. I'll put them off a day or two if they can't break Delores, but then you'll have to talk to them. You think he'll go for Mae?"

"He's a wacko, Phil. I don't know what he'll do, but I'll get on it. Can you put anyone on her to be sure?'

"Out of my district if she stays at the ranch. And I just don't have the reasons."

"Maybe I can get Jeremy to be a houseguest at the ranch till I track Ressner down," I said.

Phil looked down and nodded.

"Hell, Phil, this is damned depressing. It's like Thanksgiving when we were kids and you and I would declare a truce long enough to go for the turkey wishbone. I'd wish for a Tris Speaker glove or a million bucks."

"And I'd wish to be a cop," he said.

We sat silently in the room for about two minutes listening to the chicken yard outside the thin wooden partition. I was trying to think of an insult to get Phil going again when Seidman pushed open the door without knocking.

"Veldu's prisoner just had an accident," he said evenly. "Fell down in the interrogation room. He's out. Doesn't look so good."

"Coming," said Phil, pushing back from the desk. "Call the hospital. Have them send an ambulance just in case."

"Already did," Seidman said, closing the door.

Phil eased his cop's gut around the desk and took one lumbering step to the door. I got up behind him.

"Phil," I whispered. "Face it. You're getting too old for this stuff."

His elbow shot back and caught me in the stomach, taking my wind with a gasp. He grabbed me by the neck before I sunk to the floor and pulled our faces even closer together than Veldu and the kid had been.

"Listen, brother of mine," he hissed. I could smell the morning coffee on his breath, see life coming to his eyes. "There's a line you don't go over. Never. You just put your foot on it. Now back away." He shook me a little and stood me up. "You've got two days. That's all I can hold the state cops for. Then they get your hind end."

He let me go and I took one step backward, pulling in air and holding the wall to keep from falling. Seidman stepped back in and looked at me.

"You all right?" he said.

"Couldn't be better," I gasped.

"You woke him up," Seidman said, nodding his head toward where my brother had departed.

"It's surprising what you can accomplish with a little brotherly love and battery acid on your tongue," I sputtered, holding my stomach.

Seidman hurried off, and I staggered to the door and out. The walk through the squad room was long. I didn't want to hold my stomach, and I didn't feel like getting into a conversation about sugar rationing.

I put one hand on a desk to steady myself before making the last half-dozen steps to the door. It turned out to be Cawelti's always neat and polished desk, and his thin voice whispered in my ear, "Get your fingers off my desk or you're going to be a one-handed typist."

I got my fingers off, look at him, crossed my eyes, and gave him a Harpo Marx gookie face. Cawelti's face turned bright red, the red in a ripe sugar beet or a Walt Disney cartoon. His holster bounced with the rapid beating of his heart as he stood up.

The two women, one with the black eye and the other with the ear bandage, paused with the wino to look at us. I turned my back and walked to the door, expecting a bullet, another dent in my skull, or teeth in my neck.

"It's coming to you soon, Peters," Cawelti said.

"I understand your draft notice is in the mail, John," I said, opening the door. "We'll all miss you." And out I went.

It had, so far, been one beautiful morning and the day had just begun. When I got down to the desk, Coronet was talking to the sailor, who was now awake.

"I ought to know Jean Harlow when I see her," the kid said. "I seen all her pictures."

"Dead is dead," said Coronet reasonably between chews of his gum. "I tell you the whole ambience is out of touch, son."

I handed the kid the stick of Dentyne that Coronet had given me earlier. He looked at me suspiciously, took the gum, and said thanks.

The rain had stopped but it was coming back soon. I found a nearby drugstore open, sat at the counter, and had spaghetti Milanese and a Spur cola for twenty cents. It was early for lunch, but my stomach needed settling and my mind needed stimulation.

The waitress, who was listening to Walter Winchell on the radio, paused long enough to give me change for some phone calls and I went to work.

The first call was to Mae West.

Dizzy or Daffy answered the phone and got Mae West on a few seconds later. She breathed deeply two or three times before panting "Hel-lo Peters. What can I do for you or vice versa?"

"You can stay home for a few days and let that friend of mine, Jeremy, keep you company till we track down this Ressner. He's getting a bit unruly."

"Jeremy that big, big fella?" she asked.

"The same."

"I'd love to spend a day or two discussing the finer things in life with him. Send him down with a change of pajamas and a bad book. I'm going through a bit of divorce and can use the company of an intellec-tual."

"I'll tell him."

"Be careful."

"I try to be," I said, fidgeting for coins for my next call.

"I doubt it," she said and hung up.

I reached Jeremy in his apartment, the only apartment in the Farraday Building. He didn't like to leave the place even on Sunday. He had been working on some poems for his forthcoming anthology, an anthology that he decided to publish himself using Alice Palice's portable printing press, for which Alice would receive a month's free rent. He quickly agreed to spend a few days guarding Mae West, however.

"I think Alice has a yen for you, Jeremy," I said, counting my remaining coins.

"She is not without charm," he said. "That is a woman who never dissembles."

"And Mae West?"

"There is an art to dissembling that she has mastered," he said seriously. "I've just reworked one of the last poems for the collection. Would you like to hear it?"

"Sure," I said, standing in a Rexall drugstore, my sore stomach full of spaghetti Milanese and worrying about an escaped lunatic. I really did want to hear it, though I never understood Jeremy's poems. There was something soothing in them, like a lullaby.

"When the red slayer coughed,
I laughed
and warned him that the night air
was not his lair.
His yellow fire eyes met mine
and gave a sign
that told me I knew not what subtle ways
an ailing God's maze
is laid out in the corridors of time,
by the minions in mime.
Respect what you do not understand,
and bend or break,
he belched and he was right.
I embraced the night."

"Beautiful, Jeremy," I said.

"It's best if you've read Emerson," he said seriously.

"Best," I agreed.

"Still needs a little work," he said.

"A little," I agreed. "Maybe Mae West will give you some ideas."

I had the operator get me the number on Winning's business card. There was no answer. I told her to keep ringing. No answer. I went back to the counter, had a cup of coffee and a stale sinker, and talked to the waitress about the weather and her sister, who was pulling in big bucks working a shipyard. I was careful not to ask if she was working in the yard or on the workers in the yard.

"I'd go to the shipyards, but I haven't got the build," she confided.

She looked a little like an egg with long hair. We listened to Winchell race on about the rubber shortage and the possibility of Hitler asking for a peace meeting. Then I excused myself to try for Winning again. This time he answered after ten rings.

"Doc," I said, "we've got a problem."

I told him about Grayson and chasing Ressner. I told him there wasn't enough in the file to go on. After he got over worrying about who would pay the bill for Ressner, now that Grayson was gone, he told me a few more things about Ressner that might help.

"This is information given in confidence of an analytical session," he said and hesitated before going on, "but under the circumstances, I think . . ."

"So do I," I said. "I'm running out of coins. Shoot."

"Ressner's most recent obsession focused on Miss West, Cecil B. De Mille, and Richard Talbott, the actor."

"I know who Talbott is," I said, lining up my few remaining nickels and hoping he'd go on. "Academy Award nomination this year for *Fire on Deck*. You suggesting that I get to De Mille and Talbott?"

"I'm informing," Winning said. "I suppose Mrs. Grayson will continue to want adequate care for her former husband."

"Seems reasonable," I said, "especially after he just murdered her present husband and landed her in a golden widow's sea of Poodle piss."

"You know what Freud said about scatology, Mr. Peters?"

"No," I said, "but if I don't hang up, I'm probably going to find out. Am I still on the case?"

"You are. Report to me or my secretary daily."

"Will do," I agreed, and the operator come on to ask me for another dime. I hung up, went out, and left a ten-cent tip with the egg-shaped waitress dreaming of shipyards.

I knew where I would be going in the afternoon, but I had a stop to make this morning. I could either hit De Mille or Talbott. I settled on De Mille because I knew where he lived. It was no great secret. Every Hollywood tour took in the De Mille house and had since about 1915 or 1916. I had seen it when I was a kid with my old man on one of those days out we had together.

I got a cab and was at the De Mille house before noon. It was a big white, Spanish-looking place with awnings over the downstairs windows and glass doors all over the place that could be kicked down by a Little Rascal.

I noticed that there were plenty of lush bushes to hide behind. The sky was rumbling again, and I went through the gate trotting to beat the rain and protect my suit. A man was running toward me down the path to head me off. He ambled forward, holding a round metal hat on his head. He was, I could see even at this distance of twenty yards, about sixty, putting on a little weight but moving with a straight back and military bearing.

"And where might you be headed young man?" came the familiar radio voice.

"I'm coming to see you, Mr. De Mille," I said.

He stopped a few feet in front of me, removed his metal hat, and looked at me. He was dressed in a white shirt, poplin brown jacket, and matching pants.

"I'm afraid—" he said, the way he did on the Lux Radio Theater when time was running out.

"So am I," I jumped in. "My name's Peters, Toby Peters. I work for Dr. Robert Winning, and I'm here about someone who has escaped from Dr. Winning's institute, a Jeffrey Ressner, who you may remember."

"Remember him indeed," said De Mille, thumping his metal helmet with his fingers. "Please come into the house before the rain starts. I was just on my rounds to check the neighborhood. I'm an air-raid warden for this sector, but it can wait awhile."

We got to a side door of the massive place just as the rain came darkly down. He led the way, and I followed through glass doors into some kind of study. The floor was wood and the rug a white animal fur that seemed almost lost in the middle. There were two old leather sofas and a leather chair. They were all such a dark brown that they might as well have been black. Various gadgets sat on shelves around the room. I recognized a globe made of wire, but the others made little sense. One looked like a minature guillotine. De Mille put his helmet down, leaned against the desk, and looked at me. He picked up a square, highly polished green piece of stone, rubbed it with his thumb, and looked at me again.

"Now, Mr. Peters, what seems to be the difficulty with Mr. Ressner now? And please have a seat."

I sat in one of the leather sofas so that I could face him. His thin hair was white and the top of his bald head slightly freckled. He had a good healthy tan and eyes that wouldn't stop probing.

"Ressner got out and it looks as if he killed a man," I said.

"Indeed," said De Mille without blinking.

"He has also harassed Mae West," I went on, "and there is, of course, some chance that he will consider seeing you. He hasn't, has he?"

De Mille put the shiny stone down, walked over to touch the metal globe, and said clearly in that voice that sounded almost English, "Not for more than five years. On that last occasion, he appeared from beneath our dinner table and ranted on about playing Christ in one of my films. I brought him in here away from my family, humored him till the police arrived. He took it as an act of betrayal."

"And you haven't heard from him since?"

"I've just said no," De Mille said with a touch of irritation. "Actually, the man did have a certain uncontrolled talent that would have translated well on film. Had he sanely come to me, perhaps through an agent, I probably could have made use of him, not as Christ but as some kind of madman. And you young man, have you ever acted?"

"Not professionally," I said.

"Interesting," replied De Mille, looking at me intently. "I'm thinking of putting together a film about Dr. Wassel. Have you heard of him? The president mentioned him on the radio last month."

I said no and De Mille went on: "A great unsung hero of this war. There are many heroes of this war whose stories will never be told."

"I'd like to arrange for a police guard on the house," I said. "Just in case."

De Mille awoke from his dreams of Wassel and looked at me with a look he probably reserved for insubordinate assistants.

"While I may not be a young man any longer," he said, "I have military training and the confidence that I am able to protect my own home with my own people. I am neither a fool nor a coward, Mr. Peters, and I shall take all proper precautions. If need be, I'll have a few Paramount guards assigned to the house when I am away."

"Good idea," I said. "Frank McConnell is a good man."

"A good man, indeed," agreed De Mille with interest. "You are well acquainted with studio security."

"Used to be in the business," I said. "Who are your closest neighbors?"

"Only one," said De Mille, glancing toward the window. "W. C. Fields in the next house. We are not particularly close, though we are cordial. There was a tragedy involving my young grandchild not too long ago in Mr. Field's pool. And while it was not his fault, it is painful . . ."

"Sorry," I said.

"I want to make it clear to you that I do not usually disclose either my personal life or feelings to outsiders," he continued, looking for something to play with with his nervous fingers. "I do, however, have great concern for my family and will do whatever is needed. I will, of course, check your credentials."

"Please," I said. "Check with Mae West, or Lieutenant Phil Pevsner of the L.A.P.D., Homicide, out of Wilshire, or even Gary Cooper. He's worked with you, and I did a job for him last year."

"I shall," said De Mille, taking a step toward me. "On Wednesday we're having a war bond party at Paramount. That will be in the morning. Providing your credentials check out, you are welcome to come and perhaps discuss whatever progress you might be making."

He shook his head, leading me to the study door.

"With all the madness in the world, we surely don't need more," he said. "Perhaps you can find this Ressner and someone can help him. God knows we can use the support of our fellow men. None of us is without blemish. I'll tell you a little story."

The rain had slowed but not stopped. He went to the desk, picked up the phone, and told someone to bring the car around to the study. Then he returned to me.

"The Academy of Motion Picture Arts and Sciences has never deemed me qualified to receive its award for direction," he said, moving to my side. "They did, however, ask me to present the award this year for best direction to John Ford for his beautiful and touching *How Green Was My Valley*. Well, at the dinner, one of the distinguished guests was the ambassador of China, the country for which our hearts bleed as it suffers at the hands of Japan. When I introduced the ambassador, I spoke with emotion of the honor of his presence at the gathering and concluded by saying, 'Ladies and gentlemen, His Excellency, the Japanese ambassador.' I corrected my error too late and compounded it later that evening during the presentation to John Ford, a navy commander, whom I addressed as Major Ford. On the way home that night, my wife remarked, 'Well Cecil, at last you have done something that Hollywood will remember.' While I can display some amusement about that night now, I'd like to do something that Hollywood will indeed remember, perhaps a film tribute to our fighting men, a tribute I can best complete if our Mr. Ressner does not interfere."

He led me to the door and opened it. A car pulled up and De Mille shook my hand.

"The driver will take you wherever you are going," he said. "Take care and let me know how it comes out."

"Can I suggest that you keep these doors locked?" I said, stepping into the drizzle.

"Would it really do any good?" he said with a smile.

"Probably not," I shrugged, "but we don't like to make it easy for our enemies."

"Indeed not," agreed De Mille with a genuine smile. "I'll keep them locked."

I had the driver take me to my office. The Farraday was dark and reasonably silent on a Sunday afternoon. I opened the front door with my key and went through the dark lobby, trying to keep my mind on Ressner and the case, but knowing where it was headed. I went up the stairs in near darkness and fumbled at the door to Shelly's and my office. Inside I hit the lights and listened to my footsteps move across the floor.

A note was pinned to my cubbyhole door. I tore it down and saw that Shelly had scrawled, "What do you think of it?"

"It" was an ad torn from a newspaper. The ad was no more than an inch high and one column wide. In the top of it was a drawing of a tooth with lines sticking out around it like the lines kids make to show the sun's rays. The ad copy read:

DR. SHELDON MINCK, D.D.S., S.D.
DENTAL WORK WITH THE PAIN REMOVED
A Clean Healthy Mouth Is Your Patriotic Duty
Appointments Now Being Taken
Very Reasonable Rates For All
Discounts For Servicemen, Their Families,
City Employees and The Aged

The ad closed with our address and phone number. I went into my office and dropped it on my desk.

I had the number for Grayson's in Plaza Del Lago and I tried it.

It rang and rang and rang, but I held on. Eventually a voice, male and serious, came on.

"Grayson residence," he said.

"Miss Ressner, please, or Miss Grayson, whatever she wants to call herself," I said.

"Are you a reporter?" the man's quivering bass voice demanded.

"No, a suspect. My name is Peters. Just tell her, cowboy, and let her decide if she wants to talk to me."

"You're the one who killed Harold," he spat.

"I didn't kill Harold or anyone else. Just put Delores on and go back to whatever you were doing. This is my nickel, remember."

The phone went down hard on wood, and I waited. Out the window the sun peeked through a couple of clouds, didn't like what it saw, and went back in again. Delores came on the phone.

"Hello," she said, full of confidence.

"Were you going to tell them the truth at some point, or are you planning to let me hang for your father's crime?" I said sweetly.

"I don't know what you're talking about. You—"

"The L.A. cops and I are going to find your old man, and it won't be long. We have enough on the time of death from the coroner, the questions about the stolen Packard, and the fact that his fingerprints are on the knife to nail him."

"There were no fingerprints on the knife. The police said . . ." Somebody was kibitzing behind her, but she shushed him.

"Maybe not," I agreed. "But if you keep this up, when we grab your old man and crack this, you are going to be in trouble as an accessory to murder. I'm having a bad day, maybe a bad decade, and I'm in the mood to trample people who try to make it worse. It's raining here. I lost my car. I've got no money and I'm damn mad, lady. You want to go down with your old man, it's your bingo card to play."

"I'll think about it," she said, breaking slightly.

"Think fast," I said. "If I get him before I hear from you, it's too late." I gave her my phone number and hung up.

There wasn't much else I could do to stall. I kept a Gillette razor in the bottom drawer. I'd already shaved in the morning, but I wanted to be sure. I took it out to Shelly's sink along with a frayed toothbrush. There was plenty of sample toothpaste and powder around the office. I picked up a blue and white tin of Doctor Lyon's.

The sink was still piled high with dishes, and a spider was busily setting up house. I murdered him and set aside a razor and brush. I took off my jacket, rolled up my sleeves, and went to work. Using tooth powder for soap, I had the dishes shiny in ten minutes. I considered doing the whole office, looked at my watch, which told me nothing, and decided that I couldn't stall anymore if I was going to make it.

I shaved, dried myself with a reasonably clean towel, brushed my teeth, and got the caked paste out of the brush with hot water. At that point, someone knocked at the outer office door. I yelled "Come in" and he did. He was about six feet tall, short sandy hair, glasses, a nice suit and a little briefcase under his arm. He looked like an up-and-coming young movie star, the kind of actor you'd expect to see standing next to Robert Taylor as they defended the Pacific.

"Mr. Peters?" he asked stepping in.

I told him he was right, walked into my office, and pointed to the chair on the other side of the desk. He sat, adjusted his glasses and tie, and looked at me.

"I know what you're thinking," he said.

I had been thinking that if he was a client desperate enough to look me up on a Sunday I would do my best to get a reasonable advance out of him and put him aside for a few days.

"You were wondering why I'm not in the services," he said. "I have an ulcer in my colon."

"Sorry to hear that, Mr.—"

"Gartley," he finished reaching into his portfolio and pulling out some papers.

"What can I do for you, Mr. Gartley?" I asked folding my hands on the desk and giving him my most professional look.

"Though I'm not in the services"—Gartley went on finding the right papers—"I am doing work essential to the war effort. What does a war require?"

"Men, guns, an enemy," I answered.

"Money, Mr. Peters," he said shaking some of his papers at me. "Money. And I help to get it."

"You're raising money, selling bonds?" I guessed.

He shook his head no.

"We have written to you several times but you haven't responded," he said the way you talk to a kid who hasn't eaten all of his peas.

"We?" I tried.

"Bureau of Internal Revenue," he said sadly. "You owe your government some money. Your income tax forms were, at best, a mess."

"I never got your letters," I said looking for something to play with. I found a mechanical Eversharp pencil that hadn't worked for years.

"Possible, but unlikely. According to our records you made only one thousand eight hundred sixty-seven dollars in 1941. Is that true?"

"True."

"Forgive me, Mr. Peters, but that is a bit difficult to believe."

"I forgive you. I also agree with you. It's difficult to believe. Look around. I have a luxury office in a select location, drive the latest in modern transportation, have a standing reserved table at Ciro's and Chasen's, and reside among the stars. Drop by my house later. I'll have the servants prepare a picnic on the patio."

"You are being sarcastic," Gartley said without smiling.

"I'm trying," I agreed. "Now where do we go?"

"You give us a detailed listing of all your property and a more complete set of data on your purchases and expenditures." He handed me about seven pages of forms with spaces and lines and Internal Revenue Service written in the upper-right-hand corner.

"And if I don't?"

"You will be prosecuted for failure to cooperate with the federal government. In wartime that can be a quite serious offense."

"I have no money," I said standing up and turning my pockets inside out, which was a mistake, since I did have some change that went flying. Gartley had seen it all before. He simply looked at me, readjusted his glasses, and began putting papers back in his briefcase.

"It is difficult for us to understand," he said evenly as I sat down without bothering to push my inside-out pockets back in, "how someone with the clients you had last year, some of our most reliable and wealthy citizens, could have so little income."

"I'll explain," I said twisting the Eversharp so that the little piece of metal at the end stuck out. "If I'm lucky, I work maybe a month or two each year on cases that pay reasonably well. That's four to eight weeks. Outside of that I take odd jobs at store openings, busy hotels, picking up on bad debts. I made more when I was a guard or a cop."

"Then," Gartley said quite reasonably as he rose, "why don't you go back to those occupations?"

"I like what I'm doing," I said.

Gartley looked around the room, shrugged, and said, "You have one week to turn those papers in. You could and probably should put down a good-faith payment of a hundred dollars, which will be returned to you should our investigation of your form so indicate."

"I haven't got a hundred dollars. I haven't got a decent suit. I'm not sure if I can pay my rent next month and I need some new socks."

Gartley nodded and left. I looked at the forms. They gave me a headache. I considered trying to fill them in while I was sitting there, but the Eversharp didn't work and I couldn't find a pencil. Besides, I had something else on my mind.

It was raining. Maybe I couldn't get a cab. Maybe I couldn't get there in time. Maybe I should work on the case, go to see Mae West, head for Talbott.

Enough. I turned off the lights and went to the door. The Farraday hummed at me, and I walked down slowly. By the time I hit the front door, the rain had stopped again. The streets were wet, and a cab was cruising at about three miles an hour. I stepped out and motioned for him. He made a lazy U-turn and came to me.

I got in and told him where to take me. I hadn't brought a present. I had given Alcatraz to Phil. I could have stopped at a drugstore or flower shop, but what the hell. Whatever I got she wouldn't like. What do you give your ex-wife when she's getting married? You give her a kiss goodbye, that's what.

The trip should have taken twenty minutes to the Beverly Wilshire. It probably did, but it felt like five minutes. I got off at the hotel, paid the Sunshine cabbie, and went in. The doorman smiled when I asked where the Howard wedding was being held. Everyone smiled me into the right room. It was big. It was money. It was Howard and TWA.

The ceremony had already begun when I stepped into the room. There were about sixty people seated, watching. Anne was dressed in a brown suit, her favorite color, and Ralph was wearing a matching brown. His white hair was Vitalis smooth as he put the ring on her finger.

I couldn't tell what denomination the clergyman performing the ceremony was. It didn't matter. It was legal and it was over. Ralph kissed her, and they turned to face the guests. Anne's eyes were moist and she caught me at the door. She gave me a small smile and I nodded and smiled back.

I'd lost my Buick and my wife in twenty-four hours. Maybe, if I really worked on it, I could lose my health or my life in the next twenty-four. Something touched my sleeve. I looked at my side but no one was there. Then I looked down at Gunther.

"I thought, perhaps," he said softly, "that you might like a nearby friend."

CHAPTER 6

A woman with a sickly purple dress and tears in her eyes rushed for the happy couple, threw her arms around Ralph's neck, and began to laugh and cry. Others joined her with greater restraint, congratulating Ralph and Anne, who looked over them with a pleasant smile in my direction.

I wanted to think that her look across the crowded room was one of regret and nostalgia. I knew it probably had a tinge of fear in it. A scene of some sort was a distinct possibility, but I wasn't planning one. My only thought was to feel sorry for myself, give Anne a little guilt, and needle Ralph if I got the chance. Then I had a killer to catch.

Anne excused herself and came through the small crowd in my direction. She looked full and beautiful as she took my hand with a smile. Gunther faded back a dozen steps.

"What are you pulling, Toby?" I could see that her grin was fixed and false.

"Pulling?" I said innocently. "Nothing. You invited me. I'm here."

"Why did you bring a midget?" she whispered. The purple lady had pulled away from the cluster around Ralph and now took Anne's arm and gushed, "I hope you'll be happy, so happy with Ralph. He deserves it."

"Gunther is not a midget," I explained. "He's a little person and my friend. I told him about the wedding, and he thought I should have a friend with me."

Anne glanced at the immaculate Gunther and then at me as a

waiter with red eyes and a runny nose offered us some sparkling drinks on a tray. Anne took one, sipped, spilled a little, and laughed lightly.

"Don't embarrass me here, Toby. Don't do it."

The warning in her voice, beyond her fine white smiling teeth, was clear and present. I wondered what she had to threaten me with.

"You mean," I said, Grabbing a handful of tiny, crustless white bread sandwiches with something green inside them from a passing tray, "you won't invite me to your next wedding?"

I gulped a finger sandwich or two, turned to watch Gunther accepting a drink from the stooping waiter, and listened to Anne say, "I think it would be best if you kissed my cheek and walked out of my life now. I invited you for one reason only, to make it clear to you that you are no longer part of . . ."

Ralph had broken out of his circle of well-wishers and had stepped beaming next to Anne with a curious look at me.

"Ralph," she said, her voice showing a little strain as she reached up to wipe a stain from the corner of his mouth, "This is Toby."

Ralph's sincere small smile didn't flicker. He put out his right hand and shook mine firmly. I gobbled the last of the sandwiches.

"I'm glad you came, Toby," he said in a deep baritone. "Anne's told me a lot about you, almost all of it quite sympathetic. I admire you in many ways."

"Thanks," I said, trying not to sound sullen.

"Haven't I seen you . . . ?" he began.

"In the hall outside of Anne's apartment a few months back," I said. "We had just had a tumble when you rang. I had to throw my pants on and run."

Ralph shook his head and put his arm around Anne's shoulder. His hair was perfect. It was probably done by the Westmores.

"That doesn't serve you well, Toby. May I call you Toby?"

"Sure, may I call you Mr. Howard?"

"Toby," sighed Anne. "Please go now."

People kept sticking their head into the conversation to say congratulations or have a good honeymoon. I folded my hands in front of me and tried not to act like an ass, but the moon would probably be full that night, and I wanted to go out with a bang.

"Howard?" I said. "I think the Three Stooges are named Howard, aren't they? You related?"

Ralph looked at me as if I were a pathetic puppy who had just been caught peeing on the new carpet. I felt like it.

"Toby," Anne sobbed, clutching Ralph's hand.

"Hold it," I said. "Let's stop it there. I'm sorry. I'm a bad loser. I'll get out. If you ever need . . . well, if you."

I blew out some air, shrugged at Anne and Ralph, and turned to leave. Gunther was waiting for a sign from me. He put down his almost finished drink and stepped in my direction.

"Toby," Anne said softly. "Take care of yourself."

I put up my right hand and waved. It would make a nice parting gesture. Tragic, shoulders down. I felt better. The purple lady caught me at the door and kissed my cheek.

"Your sister is beautiful," she sobbed.

"Right," I said and hurried out the door with Gunther at my side.

We went to Gunther's car without a word and said nothing for five blocks.

"He seems a decent person," Gunther tried.

"Right."

"Don't you want her to be happy?"

"I don't know."

We were quiet for four more blocks then and I said, "Yeah, I want her to be happy."

"Which means?" Gunther prompted.

"I stay out of their life."

I tried to talk to Gunther into stopping for tacos. I wanted to drown my grief in half-a-dozen tacos and a gallon of Pepsi. Gunther said he would go, but he couldn't hide the revulsion, It wasn't the tacos as much as the places I liked to eat them. I told him to forget it, and we went back to the boardinghouse, where we had dinner in my room prepared by Gunther: tuna and cheese sandwiches with a bottle of wine Gunther had saved from last Christmas.

Gunther listened to my tale of Ressner and the Grayson murder and commented that the sun, if it ever came out, might improve my outlook on life.

My outlook wasn't improved by Mrs. Plaut barreling through my door with a new chapter of her never-ending book on her family. Mrs. Plaut was convinced that I was an editor and part-time exterminator. She wasn't sure whether I exterminated rats, mice, and bugs or people or both. She really didn't care as long as I paid my fifteen dollars-a-month rent, read her manuscript, and didn't destroy her furniture. She had, over the past year, removed almost every doily, photo, and handmade item from my room to protect them from the odd assortment of visitors who tramped through.

"Mr. Gunther, Mr. Peelers," she said in a very businesslike way. She clutched the pages to her nonexistent bosom and pursed her lips before placing the pages on the corner of the table where we were sitting.

"Cousin Dora's Indian attack," she said, patting the stack of papers.

"Cousin Dora was attacked by Indians." I said sympathetically.

"Cousin Dora attacked the Indians," she corrected. "It's all in here. There are some in the family, particularly Uncle Tucker, who opined that the Indians had it coming. Others thought otherwise."

"Really," I said, downing the rest of my glass of celebration wine and holding it out for a refill from Gunther.

"Dora, you must know, was not really a cousin by birth but by marriage. I leave it to you to decide." She pulled her cloth robe around her and glanced at the nearly empty wine bottle.

"Would you like a small glass, Mrs. Plaut?" I asked gallantly.

"No," she said, "but I'll have a small glass of wine."

Gunther climbed off the chair, found a reasonably clean glass, and poured. Mrs. Plaut downed it.

"Your comments and suggestions will as always be greatly appreciated," she said and left.

A few minutes later Gunther said goodnight. I did the dishes, finished the wine, raced Mr. Hill the accountant for the bathroom, lost, and went back to my room to read about Cousin Dora:

> Oh, said Cousin Dora or something like that I don't know for sure, the Indians are coming. And they were, a ragmuffin band of six or so from near Yuma. They came every Saturday like railroad men to trade pelts and empty bottles to Uncle Tucker for whatever he would give, which was not always much but neither were the pelts. Uncle Tucker was known to opine that some of the pelts belonged not to fox but to animals of a lesser ilk. In fact he said some of the pelts might be those of cows reported missing from the farm of the Grangers who lived the other side of the ridges.

Cows are strange creatures. Just recently a cow in Minnesota was given a special supply of sugar by President Roosevelt to cure its insanity.

When the Indians came through the door they were feeling mean because they had no bottles and only a few pelts.

Uncle Tucker said he would trade them a pig but not the pig named Homer, which Cousin Dora talked to, but one of the other pigs that had no name and if traded would not be likely to get one.

The Indians hemmed and hawed as Indians used to do before they made the trade and left but not before one of them either did or did not make a lewd suggestion to Cousin Dora who was particularly attractive to Indians because she was fat and some Indians like women who are fat but not sassy. Cousin Dora was sassy. The Indian was just paying a stupid compliment I would think but Cousin Dora did not so think. She entreated him to remain for supper and so he did because he didn't want to miss a free meal though he might have thought different had he tasted Aunt Jessica's cooking which was reputed not the best in the family though probably within bounds in Arizona. The other Indians went and after dinner this one wanted to leave too but he was considerable smaller than Cousin Dora and Uncle did not have a mind to quarrel with her.

I don't quarrel with God or Cousin Dora he said often sometimes when it made little or no sense but this time it did. The Indian tried to get away but it weren't any use. Dora sat him down and told him the run of things and he understood mostly. Here the story diverges. Uncle Tucker, whose mind went to putty in 1916, remembered that the Indian wanted to go most strongly. Aunt Jessica remembered only his weeping and talking strange. Cousin Dora simply confessed when asked that she kidnapped the Indian who she said was named Ira Glick. I do not think that was really his name though it may have sounded something like it in Indian.

Next day when the other Indians came back and requested the return of Ira Glick Uncle Tucker was in a mood to argue since it was only God and Cousin Dora he didn't quarrel with. He didn't mind quarreling with Indians, peddlers and Aunt Jessica. He was even heard to quarrel with the mule though he denied in later years that he did anything but scold the animal in detail.

The Indians said they would not leave without Ira Glick but Cousin Dora said no no you must leave without Ira Glick. He is staying. They got mad and talked Indian according to all accounts and said they would be back with something that would change the mind even of Cousin Dora. They reckoned without Cousin's stubborn nature inherited by her through her father's side of the family and not through the Plauts.

Dora fled with Ira and was not heard of again for seven years when she returned and demonstrated three offspring which to hear tell displayed the worst of both the savage and the cousin. All three were fat and red of face and lolled around till even Uncle Tucker said enough since Aunt Jessica refused to speak to Dora and threw them out.

The last we in the family heard of Dora Glick she was reported to have been sheep ranching near the Pecos and that Ira Glick had run away but had not joined his tribe. Some, not Uncle Tucker and that is for sure, say Ira Glick went into the political business and became governor of Arizona just before it achieved statehood. I do not think Indians can be governor but they may have thought him to be Jewish with such a name.

When I woke up the next morning, the sun was shining, the pages were scattered all around the floor. Since they weren't numbered, I didn't worry about the order. I picked them up, tapped them straight, and placed them on the sofa.

I brushed my teeth and tongue, shaved, breakfasted on Shreddies mixed with Wheaties, dressed, and told myself that I had a killer to find and maybe a murder to prevent. But first I had a car to buy.

I took a Monday morning bus with the people going to work late and got to Arnie's by ten. He was in his oil-smelling office screwing something into a glob of metal.

"How much for the '38 Ford without a trade? My Buick died in the desert."

A customer pulled in with a big black car and honked his horn. It was loud. Arnie lifted his eyes to the customer, waved, and kept on fiddling.

"Two twenty," he said. "That's a favor, since you've got no trade-in."

"I've got eighty, a fee coming in from a client back East, and a job I'm working on," I said.

Arnie put down his screwdriver, rubbed a little more grease on his nose, and looked indecisive.

"I can sell that baby just like that," he said. "She's no carroodi."

The customer, a well-dressed guy with a briefcase, looked at his watch and did his best to spread exasperation through the neighborhood.

"Arnie, have we got a deal or not?"

Arnie gave a massive groan that I took as a false sign of defeat. He was, out of the goodness of his stone heart, going to sell me sight unseen the '38 Ford. He held out his hand. I fished out my wallet, handed him the eighty, and hoped that the twenty-five I had left would last till more came in.

"She's in back, next the the busted pump," he said, counting the money. "I'll make a receipt and stuff when I finish with flash pants over there."

The car was where he said it would be, and it didn't look too bad. The rear bumper sagged and one of the headlights looked bloodshot. In addition it was a small two-seater coupe, which Arnie had neglected to mention. There wasn't much room for baggage or passengers. The keys were under the sunshade, where mechanics always hide them. It took a little to start the Ford, but start it did and the engine sounded reasonable. The gas gauge read empty.

I pulled out slowly and drove to the front pump. Arnie was talking to Mr. Flash Pants.

"Needs gas," I yelled through the open window.

"Nah," said Arnie adjusting his baseball cap. "Gauge is broken. I filled her up."

"Can you fix it?"

"Just fill it every few days," he said. "Cost you a bundle to fix it."

At least the radio worked. I turned it on and discovered that the Japanese had shelled Corregidor for five hours, but General Wainright was holding on. I also learned that the Nazis had executed seventy-two Dutchmen for aiding the Allies and that if you want steady nerves to fly Uncle Sam's bombers across the ocean, you should smoke Camels.

By eleven I was parked in the driveway outside the home of Richard Talbott, Academy Award winner, shoo-in nominee for another in 1942 and, from what I had heard, a man who could hold his booze, but not very well.

CHAPTER 7

The chimes echoed deeply inside of Talbott's house. I looked around the grounds, which were on a slight rolling hill on Alpine just off Santa Monica Boulevard in Beverly Hills. The grass was well trimmed, the bushes neatly clipped, and the birds chirping happily in front of the big white house that dated back to the bad old days and had probably belonged to some silent film star who passed this way but once. I hit the chimes again and listened to them carom their three notes beyond the door. Then it opened.

Jeremy calls it déjà vu. He even wrote a poem with that title. I couldn't see why it didn't have a straight American name like, "Haven't I Been This Way Before?" or "(Seems to Me) I've Heard That Song Before."

The woman in a light blue dress stood in front of me with her arms folded. She was a beautiful blond named Brenda Stallings, who hadn't aged in the four years since I last saw her. She had been wearing a blue dress the first time she had greeted me just before she seduced me and later shot me in the back. I can't say it was good to see her.

"I came to return your bullet," I said.

Brenda Stallings had been a wealthy society deb about fifteen years earlier. She had doubled for Harlow, and then had a short, successful film career before marrying a blackmailing twerp actor named Harry Beaumont, who was now lying somewhere near Rin Tin Tin in Roseland cemetery. But Brenda was an actress. She didn't blink as she took a step back to let me in and said, "You may keep it if you like."

I stepped in and she closed the door. A few feet from her now I could see the changes. She was still beautiful, still had the body and the carriage, but shadows around the corner of the mouth and eyes hinted at what she had been through if someone looked close enough, which was what I was doing.

"How did you find me?" she said, walking ahead of me without looking back. He legs were great and her yellow hair still bounced softly on her neck. I'd been through it before. Yes, I had.

We stopped in a living room that looked like the set of a Fred Astaire movie, blacks and whites and keep your hands off. It was Brenda's style. I looked around for the Oscar. There were two of them on the white piano. She caught my look.

"The one on the left is Richard's for *Captain Daring*," she said. "The other," she went on walking over to it and touching something on the back, "you may recall." Flames spurted out of the Oscar's gold head. She picked up a cigarette from a gold box on the piano, lit it, and put the Oscar back.

"I recall."

Her cold blue eyes looked at the burning end of her cigarette and then at me.

"Please." She pointed at the various pieces of furniture, and I tried to figure out which one I'd be least likely to leave a stain on. I could have gone to the piano bench, which was also white, but I can't play the piano and I'd feel silly. I sat on the white arm of an overstuffed chair.

"I'm looking for Richard Talbott," I explained. "He does live here, doesn't he?"

She nodded and smoked staring at me. She wasn't going to make it easy. As I recalled, I had done her a reasonably good turn when last we met, but she wasn't the kind to show gratitude, or weakness, or much of anything if she could help it.

"He lives here and so do I," she said, reaching for a gold ashtray.

"I live in Hollywood in Mrs. Plaut's Boardinghouse," I said, looking around and finding two huge painted portraits on the wall over the doorway we had entered. One was of Brenda Stallings, bronzed and queenly in white. It had been in her old house, not too far from here. The other portrait was Richard Talbott wearing a blue pea coat with a robust, healthy tooth-filled smile. Brenda had done her best to make the house and Talbott her own. In the old house the portrait had been of Harry Beaumont. If my memory served me right, there was a superficial similarity between Beaumont and Talbott.

"How's Lynn?" I tried, looking at Brenda with my best party smile. Lynn was her daughter who now must be, hell about nineteen or twenty.

Brenda put out her cigarette and dropped lazily into the armchair across from me. She had done that too when I first met her. It was, I decided, a scene she played well and did over and over.

"Lynn is fine," she said. "We don't see much of each other. She's in New York going to school and seriously interested in a not-too-young producer. What do you want with Richard?"

"I thought I'd save his life," I said.

"Would you like a drink?" she came back.

"Water with ice would be fine."

"Will lemonade do?"

"Sure."

Brenda eased herself out of the chair and took a leisurely trip across the black-and-white checkerboard rug and out of the room. I heard her off somewhere giving orders in something that might have been Spanish. She was back in a few seconds.

"Carlotta will bring your drink in a few moments," she said, going to the piano, picking up another cigarette, and putting it back down again. She was nervous. Maybe it was me, seeing me again and remembering some bad times. Maybe it was something else.

"Has Talbott had any threats?" I asked. "Any problems?"

"Richard's primary threats are to his liver, and his primary problem is his capacity to serve as a receptacle for the entire importation of scotch into California." She smiled prettily as she spoke and searched for something to fiddle with.

"Lady, you are a real expert in picking your men," I said.

"I do seem to have a certain talent for it, don't I?"

"Talbott," I said.

"Yes, Richard." Her sigh lifted her breasts under her dress and demanded my attention. It was her scene, and I let her play it. "He and a producer are out for a late-morning business session at one of Richard's favorite bars, of which there are several within vomiting distance." She looked out the window and then up at her portrait and touched her hair before going on. "It's some sort of big foreign deal, and I doubt if they will be back for some time. Do you plan to tell me what it's all about? This scene could stand cutting . . ."

At which point Carlotta, wearing a black dress and being very tiny, came in and handed me a tall lemonade with ice and a little smile. Brenda drank nothing. Carlotta walked out. The whole thing was very elegant, and I wasn't.

"There's a nut who's got it in for Talbott and a few other movie people, I said. She looked at me seriously.

"Richard is used to that," she said. "So are most stars."

"This one has probably killed someone."

Something hit her in the gut, and she didn't have time to be pretty about it.

"So, I'd like to find Talbott, talk to him, warn him, and maybe set up some protection for him while he stays off the streets till I catch the guy," I went on.

Brenda moved toward me. I gurgled some lemonade, which was too sweet, and looked for some place to put it without leaving a ring. There was no place. I held it.

"There was a call yesterday," she said. "Richard said it was just a stupid fan, but he was shaken by it. It might . . ."

"It might," I agreed, handing her the glass. She took it, stared at it without seeing it, and placed it on a shiny black table. "I think I'll just wait here till he gets back, if it's all right with you."

"Of course," she said. The act was dropping fast now. We had gone beyond her usual lines, and the scene wasn't going to end in a seduction or a burst of anger. Maybe I'd get a glimpse of the Brenda Stallings buried under a decade and a half of Brenda Stallings. Her pink mouth opened slightly. I remembered that pink mouth. She started to say, "Toby, Mr. Peters I—"

"Hold it," I jumped in. "This producer Talbott is with. Did he know him? I mean before."

"No," she said. "He called this morning and . . . you don't think?"

"Sometimes I do, like right now. What did the guy look like?"

I got up and walked over to her. The front was dropping fast. Her hand went to her forehead and brushed away her hair.

"I didn't see him. I was upstairs. Richard—"

"Did he have a name? The producer?"

"I'm trying to think." And she was. She pressed her hand to her forehead to urge the memory out. "Resnick, I think."

"How about Ressner," I cued her, taking her arms.

She nodded weakly.

"That's my man," I said.

"It's going to happen again," she whispered and sank against me. She felt soft and good and smelled great, but I put her down gently and fast. "Where does Talbott like to hold his meetings? Brenda, where?"

"I'm trying," she said. And she was. I backed away to give her some space. "Let's see. He's taken me to Buddy's on Gower, the Manhattan off Fairfax, Trinity's American on Hollywood Boulevard, the—"

"I'll start with those," I said, "and call you if I strike out. If he checks in, tell him that Ressner is a dangerous nut and to get away from him fast, find the nearest cop, and duck. You got that?"

She nodded.

"Toby, I'm sorry I shot you."

"Apology accepted." I went out of the room and just barely danced past Carlotta, who had been eavesdropping and didn't have time to get away.

"Try the Manhattan first," she whispered.

"Gracias," I whispered back and ran out the front door and toward my new Ford.

The sky was closing in again as I pulled onto Santa Monica and tried to keep from going over the speed limit. I pushed the outer edges, flipped on the radio, which sputtered and gave me nothing, turned it off, and reached over to the glove compartment for my .38, which, of course, wasn't there but back in my room in the white box.

Traffic started to back up on me, and I didn't know how long I was taking. My watch didn't help, the radio didn't work, and my inner clock was foul. A Yellow cab with a sign on top saying GROUP RIDING IS PATRIOTIC GO YELLOW stopped abruptly in front of me and I almost plowed into him. Something did hit me from behind and the sound of metal hitting asphalt tinkled in my ear. I leaped out just as the guy who had plowed into me sped past with his head hunched down. My rear bumper lay in the street. I picked it up and shoved it into the narrow backseat through the front window. The car was too small to take the whole thing into the rear, so some of it had to stick out the passenger window.

"There are days, God," I said to myself, "when even I don't appreciate your sense of humor."

There was no parking place open on Fairfax. I hadn't expected one. I pulled in next to a fireplug, got out, and ran for the Manhattan. Outside, I pulled myself together, tried to stop panting, and stepped into the near-total darkness.

There were eight or nine people in the place. Three at the bar, the rest in booths. Even this early a guy was playing the piano and singing "It Ain't Necessarily So." I looked around for Talbott but didn't spot him. I still didn't know what Ressner looked like.

The bartender was a young guy in a red vest, white shirt, and red tie. I hurried to the bar.

"What will you have?" he said.

"Richard Talbott," I answered. "I'm from Paramount. He has an urgent message. Has he been in here today?"

The bartender looked me over, wondering about the mugs studios hired to deliver messages.

"He was here with another guy," he said.

"The other guy. What did he look like?"

The barkeep shrugged. "Dunno, kind of tall, dark glasses."

"When did they leave? Where did they go?" I pushed.

"They didn't leave," he said. "They're in the back."

The back was apparently behind some heavy velvet red drapes. I pushed away from the bar and headed for them. Behind me I heard someone at the bar calling for drinks.

Beyond the drapes was a small alcove and a narrow corridor. Just inside the corridor was a men's room and a ladies' room. Beyond that were two doors. I pushed open the first door, which led to a medium-size private room with a few tables, a bar in the corner, and chairs. The room was empty, but an amber light was on in the ceiling and a Dewar's Black Label sign glowed over the bar. I moved to the bar where two glasses stood and touched a small red liquid pool near one glass. It looked thick and brown in the light. It felt sticky and familiar.

Drops of the liquid spotted the tile floor and left a trail to the corner of the room where an emergency exit door stood. It was slightly open. I pushed it and started to step out. The sky was going black again. I had time to notice that and some vague shapes in front of me when something caught me in the stomach. Some agonized animal bellowed "Arggghh," and I had the feeling that I was being turned upside down and thrown on my back by a giant baby. Then there was nothing.

Koko the clown came and perched on my nose. Behind him someone spoke. I thought the voice said, "Too late again," but I wasn't sure. Koko grinned down at me and wanted to play.

I didn't want to play. This was it. I wasn't so far from fifty, with no money in the sock, a body that threatened to leave me, an ex-wife. . . . The hell with that. I'd gone over it before. Get up and keep going, I told myself. Koko could skate around and play tricks on Uncle Max. The Nazis and the Japs could throw what they had at us. My job was an easy one. Just get up and go back to work, but I couldn't do it. My eyes just wouldn't open. I suggested a game to Koko, sly fox that I was. If he'd open my eyes, I'd play with him. I chuckled, knowing that if he helped me open my eyes I'd be awake and I wouldn't have to play with him. I'd have a more dangerous game to play. Koko, the sucker, agreed, and my eyes opened to a bright light. I closed them again.

"This one ain't dead," an incredulous voice said.

"He's bloodier than the other one," came another voice. "You hear me fella?"

"I hear you," I said.

"What he say?" came the first voice again.

"I think he said 'I dare you,'" said the second voice. I opened my eyes again and turned from the flashlight to look into the open eyes of Richard Talbott. They were big and brown and dead, and rain was pelting his famous cheeks. So much for Brenda Stallings's luck and mine.

I tried to sit up, but hands held me back.

"You better just lie there till an ambulance comes," came the first voice, which, in the cloud-covered darkness, I could see belonged to a cop in a raincoat, a young cop.

"I'll get pneumonia lying here," I told him. "And I've got a bad back."

The second cop was not much older than the first.

"I think you better not move," he commanded.

I sat up and looked over at Talbott. There was a knife sticking out of his chest, just about where the other one had been posted in Grayson.

"You think I did this?" I said, wiping rain and blood from my face.

"I don't think anything," said the second cop. "But you're not going anywhere."

"Hell, Sol, let's get him inside," said the younger cop. "There's no point in our standing out here in the rain. If he wants to move, it's his worry."

Sol grunted and looked at me.

"O.K. You try anything and you get this flashlight across your face," Sol warned.

"Just what I need," I groaned and let them drag me through the exit door and back into the private room in the Manhattan.

They sat me on a chair and found some towels to sop up the blood in my hair. I could feel the cut but not how deep it was.

"You want to tell us what happened?" tried Sol's partner, the kid.

"No," I said "I'll just have to tell it again. Call Lieutenant Pevsner or Sergeant Seidman at the Wilshire station. They're Homicide. Tell them what you found and that I'm Toby Peters."

"You a cop?" said Sol.

"No," I said. "A victim."

"You kill that guy out there?" said the kid.

"That guy is Richard Talbott," I said, closing my eyes.

"The big actor?" Sol cried.

I nodded.

"The guy with the scythe gets 'em all," said Sol wisely.

"The long and the short and the tall," I agreed and closed my eyes, pretending to go out again.

CHAPTER 8

"Well Toby, my lad," a mellow voice broke through wherever I was dreaming, "we have a new theory about you."

I opened my eyes to the placid face above me. It was a tolerant face, the face of a man of sixty or more who had seen much and wanted to go home to a hot bath and a drink. He could have been a priest or a soldier. He could even have been a cop, but I guessed that he was a doctor. The white uniform and stethoscope around his neck were my best clues. It also helped that I recognized the emergency room at L.A. County. I'd been there often enough before.

"My name is Dr. Melanks," he said, picking up a thick file. I knew it was mine. I remembered the time Doc Parry had held it up with a shake of the head not much different from kindly Doc Melanks's. Parry was off in the Pacific somewhere seeing cases even more interesting than mine. I was used to thick files about me. I even took kind of a perverse pride in them.

"Can you hear me?" Melanks asked, rubbing the bridge of his

nose. The backs of his fingers had fine gray hairs growing at the knuckles.

"A few members of the staff now believe that the constant reign of terror to your anatomy is causing a building up of resistance by your body. Not that you are immune to damage but that your body has somehow said, 'What the hell, I can take anything.' Your skull no longer deserves the anatomical right to be referred to as a skull. We are not quite sure what to call it."

I tried to sit up and made it to one elbow. I was in a hospital gown.

"The closest thing I have seen to what we are laughingly calling your cranium belonged to a punch-drunk fighter named Ramirez who, when his career was finished, made an occasional fifty cents by battering down doors with his head. Mr. Ramirez was incapable of coherent speech by that time and seemed to think he was a robot. Are you following the allegorical level of my tale, Mr. Peters?"

"If I continue to get hit in the head, my brain will turn to Junket pudding," I said.

"Your brain is almost certainly pudding by now," said Dr. Melanks. "I simply want you to sign it over to me on your death. I am sixty-seven and suffering from arthritis, a weak heart, mild sclerosis, and a very poor hereditary profile, but I should outlive you by a comfortable margin."

He put down the chart, stepped in front of me, lifted my eyelids, shined a little flashlight into them, breathing mint in my face, and stood back.

"I'm not even going to bother to warn you," he said. "It won't do any good. I can see that Parry and a number of others have told you of the consequences of your folly. If you can rise, do so. If you can walk, amaze me with the sight. You have two dozen stitches in your head, at the base of your scalp."

"I can feel them," I said, sitting up and touching the bandage.

"A good omen," sighed Melanks. "The whole thing is free of charge, of course, on the condition that you come back here in three days to let me take the stitches out and engage in a bit of anatomical phrenology for the medical students, who should see everything at least once."

I stood and looked around for my clothes.

"Would you like to go through that door headfirst?" he said wearily. "I could sew you up again. I've already missed my dinner and part of my sleep. It would be an education to me in my declining years."

I had enough of Doc Melanks's sarcasm. What I needed was some pants before the police dropped in for a chat.

Melanks shook his head one more time and exited with a flourish and a swish of his white coat. He was followed almost immediately by Phil and Steve Seidman.

Phil had shaved since yesterday, and Seidman looked even more pale in the hospital light. Seidman leaned against the door, which he closed behind him, and Phil found a chrome-legged chair to sit on. He looked around the room as if I weren't there, admiring the table, medicine cabinet, and the poison chart on the wall. Nobody spoke. This went on for about three minutes, when I gave up.

"Ressner killed him," I said.

This started no general discussion, so I plunged forward, going to the metal cabinet in the corner to search for my clothes. They weren't there.

"Ressner's doctor told me he might go after Talbott," I said. "So I went to Talbott's house. You can check with Brenda Stallings. You remember her. Flynn case in '39. She told me Talbott was out with Ressner at the Manhattan. I went there and followed them into the back room. I just followed the trail of blood to the back door and Ressner laid me out."

"You saw Ressner?" Seidman asked.

"No, but it's the same setup as the Grayson killing, isn't it?"

Phil scratched his head and looked at his fingernails.

"I didn't kill him," I repeated.

"We don't think you did," said Seidman. Phil remained mute. "But this is going to be big news in tomorrow's paper and on the radio. You better hope the Japs make a run on Corregidor. You're all we've got and Talbott is big news. We'll throw you to the newspapers so they'll stay off our tochis for a week or so."

"Nailing me won't get you Ressner," I said. "And he'll just go after Mae West or De Mille."

"We'll put some coverage on them," said Seidman. "How much chance have you got of turning up Ressner?"

I looked at Phil, who sat in the chrome chair and listened as if he were at a private performance of a new play.

"I'll have him in twenty-four hours," I said, having no idea where Ressner might be. Hell, I didn't even know where my pants were.

"Horseshit," said Phil finally.

I gave a deep fake sigh and clutched my heart.

"Thank God," I said. "I thought the newspapers had cut out your heart."

"No," said Phil standing and stretching. His belly sagged as he took a step toward me. "Just my tongue. I asked you for a favor. I asked you to protect someone and keep things quiet. That's supposed to be what you do best. Shit, that's the only thing you can do. And look at this. A big state land developer and a movie star are dead."

"People are dying by the hundreds on both sides of the ocean" I reminded him.

"But I'm not responsible for them," said Phil, stepping in front of me. I pulled back and he went on. "I'm not going to belt you. What I'm going to do is give you twenty-four hours. Then I'm going to have to haul you in, and you're going to have to warm your toes in County if you can't make bond while we try to find Ressner, and Mae West gets dragged into this. You get my drift, brother?"

"Pulsating through my stitches," I said. "Now if you can get me a pair of pants, I'll be on my way."

"You want to let us in on this and save us all some time and grief?" asked Seidman.

"I think I'll do it my way," I said, knowing that my way was to blunder forward with my head down like Ramirez till I hit the right door. Without another word they left the room.

"My pants," I shouted after them and followed them into the hall. They kept marching right through the waiting room past the mottled crew of black, yellow, white, brown, and green people in various states of emergency. The ones who were able looked up at me. Some, no doubt, wondered why the police had taken my pants.

Back in the treatment room I went to the phone and called Mrs. Plaut's

"Hell. . . ." Mrs. Plaut started, but someone was wrestling her for the phone.

"Mr. Gunther," I heard her squeal.

Then Gunther came on. "Yes?"

"It's me, Toby," I said.

"I hoped it would be."

Behind him I heard Mrs. Plaut cry, "One more such incident, Mr. Gunther, and you shall have to pack up all your neat little clothes and get your rump out of here."

I explained my predicament to Gunther, who had been worrying about me, and he told me that he had already had my milk-stained suit cleaned and pressed and the button sewed back on. It would take him no more than fifteen minutes or so to get to the hospital.

While I waited in the room wondering what I would do next, a pair of nurses stuck their heads in. The younger of the two said, "That's him." The older one looked at me in awe and held up an X ray, which I assumed was my skull. I considered slinging something at them the way the chimps did in the zoo, but decided to preserve whatever dignity I might have left, which amounted to less than that of Huntz Hall's character in the Bowery Boys movies.

Gunther made it in sixteen minutes according to the wall clock and four minutes according to my old man's watch. I was dressed a few seconds later and signing my release papers seconds after that, with Dr. Melanks hovering over me with a cup of coffee.

"I was only half joking about having you sign your body over to me," he said. "I'd like to watch a good pathologist going at your skull."

"Bye doc," I grinned, fitting on the hat that Gunther had brought so that it rested just above the bandage at the back of my head. "Watch your blood pressure."

Gunther drove me to Fairfax, suggesting that I come home and get a good night's rest before I retrieved my car. I told him that it probably wouldn't be there if I waited till morning. The cops would have towed it away. He shrugged, stepped on his elongated gas pedal, and hurried into the night with his radio tuned to Gene Autry.

The Ford was still in front of the fireplug when we got there. It was decorated by four parking tickets. I shoved them into the glove compartment, started the engine, wondered how much gas I had used, and followed Gunther back to Hollywood. The bumper next to me bobbed up and down, scratching at the upholstery. I parked in front of Mrs. Plaut's and hauled the bumper up to my room. I couldn't sleep on my back because of the stitches. Sleeping on my stomach meant a sure backache in the morning. I propped myself on my side with pillows as a compromise and considered retirement and a new career.

Maybe Arnie could teach me the car business, or Shelly could give me a two-week course in dentistry, or Jeremy could make me the Farraday janitor, or Gunther could teach me how to speak Norwegian so I could translate the classics. Maybe. I slept surprisingly well.

CHAPTER 9

Mrs. Plaut stood over me when I opened my eyes. The Beech-Nut gum clock on the wall told me it was nine in the morning. Her teacher-folded hands and the no-nonsense tight lips above her lacy collar told me she had a problem.

"I am vexed," she said.

I tried to roll back to get a good look at her vexation, but my head touched the pillow and reminded me of my stitches. I rolled gently to a sitting position, yawned, and fixed my bleary eyes on her.

"You are vexed," I encouraged.

"First Mr. Gunther behaves with improper respect," she said, wringing her hands. "Next you confound the pages of my chapter on Cousin Dora. Did you read the chapter?"

"Cousin Dora attacked the Indians," I yawned. "The Indians fled and preserved their virtue."

"But still I am vexed," she went on. I wasn't sure if she had heard my summary. "The newspaper informs me that you are involved again in bodies. A news reporter even called this morning to speak to you. I told him that I had seen Mr. Richard Talbott in *Destiny's Darling* four or five times. That was when Mr. Richard Talbott was a young man and the movies, thank Jesus, didn't talk. He had fine hair like my brother Bernard."

"You are vexed," I reminded her loudly, pushing up from the mattress on the floor.

"Please put something on," she said. I looked down at my underwear, nodded, and reached for my pants. "I think it improper that you should have killed Mr. Talbott. That's what I have to say."

"I didn't kill him," I said, trying to force my belt one notch over.

"Good," she said, still grinding her knuckles. "The newspaper said you had been questioned concerning the crime, but it didn't say you had killed him."

"What else did the paper say?" I yelled. I pulled a nearly empty bottle of milk from the refrigerator, started the coffee, and rummaged through my cereals, finally settling on All Bran. It might be one of those days. I knew I had some brown sugar someplace but was having trouble tracking it down.

"The paper also said that," she went on obligingly, "the Japanese have stormed Corregidor, Laval has rejected President Roosevelt's warning, Great Britain is fighting the Vichy French on Madagascar, and Joe DiMaggio's triple in the tenth inning beat the Chicago White Sox."

It wasn't the subject I had in mind, but I appreciated the summary and looked out of the window. The damn sky was clear. Lord God, hallelujah.

I held up the box of All Bran for Mrs. Plaut to look at and offered to share it with her. She shook her head no.

"So, Mr. Peters, what are we going to do?"

About the Japanese, fight and pray. About DiMaggio, nothing. I wasn't a Sox fan.

"I will be much more circumspect in the future," I yelled.

This seemed to placate her. Outside I could hear footsteps.

"I am well into my chapter on the Beemer side of the family and their encounters in science," she said. "Then we should be ready to seek a publisher."

We? I nodded dumbly and poured my cereal just as the knock came at my door.

"Come in," I shouted and Gunther came in, all suited in gray.

Mrs. Plaut failed to hear him enter and continued to glare at me while I sat and ate. Gunther moved past her and caught the corner of her eye.

"Mr. Gunther," she said as he moved to the table. "You have, until yesterday, always been a perfect little gentleman. I do not know what possessed you."

"I'm truly sorry, Mrs. Plaut," Gunther said with a continental bow of his head.

"When you want to apologize," she went on, "I'll be downstairs. And Mr. Peelers, will you please remove that thing." She pointed to the bumper. With that and the Dora chapter she raced from the room.

"How might your head be this morning, Toby?" Gunther said as he poured the coffee.

"Feels like someone removed a few inches of scalp and sewed the whole thing back on too tight. Not bad though." The All Bran was just what I needed.

"You seem surprisingly good spirited," he observed, pouring himself some coffee after he recleaned the cup he had selected.

"Can't explain it," I said, pouring some more All Bran into the remaining milk in my bowl and spooning out some brown sugar, which I had found in the refrigerator. I had to dig the spoon in like a shovel to get it out. "Lost Anne. Beaten. Suspect in two murders. Broke. Income tax people are after me. War going on. But"—I held up a finger—"I am on the job."

"Toby, I am having a slight idiomatic problem again in a translation I am engaged in for radio." Gunther was serious about his translations. "In this tale, a man says 'That's the way the ball bounces.' My research indicates that this expression derives from the irregular trajectory of an American football when it strikes the ground. This is a result of the peculiar shape of the ball. Most balls bounce quite true and predictably. An English rugby ball is somewhat similar, but this translation is into French, and I am at a loss."

"Just skip it, Gunther," I advised.

"That is not professional. Do you just skip it when you are working for a client?"

"No, I guess not."

"Ah, there, so see," he said, dabbing the corner of his lips with a paper napkin. I resisted the urge to scratch my itching stomach.

"I'll think about it. I'm taking a drive up near Fresno today. Probably stay over. Want to join me?"

"I'm afraid I cannot unless you are too incapacitated to drive. I have much work, much work."

"I can make it," I said, getting up and stacking the dishes in the sink. Gunther finished the last of his coffee, eased himself from the chair, and moved past me to wash the dishes. I didn't protest.

I shaved in the communal bathroom down the hall, brushed my

furry teeth, noted the increasing amount of gray in my hair, and tried to get a look at my bandage, which just peeked out from behind my neck. There were a few aspirin left in the medicine cabinet. I think they were Hill's. I gulped them and went back to my room. Gunther was gone. I made my bed, a job that consisted of kicking at the blanket so that it covered a pillow.

A search of the room turned up enough change to make the phone calls I needed to make. The first was to Dr. Winning. He answered on the second ring.

"Mr. Peters," he said evenly. "You have found Mr. Ressner?"

"Not quite," I said. "I'm following his trail, though. He produced another corpse yesterday. Richard Talbott the actor."

There was a silence on Winning's end. Obviously, he didn't read the L.A. papers, though I would have pegged Talbott's death for national news. I waited.

"This is terrible," he finally said, which was accurate but not very imaginative. "What are you going to do?"

"Find him," I said. "I'm going to call the ex-Mrs. Ressner, the widow Grayson, and her daughter to see what I can dig up. Then I thought I'd come up and see you, maybe check Ressner's room, talk to some of the staff or patients who knew him."

More silence and then, "I'm not sure that would be wise. Many of the patients do not know Mr. Ressner is gone. The balance in a mental hospital such as ours is very delicate, very delicate."

"I'll be my most charming, doctor. I just don't have enough to go on to find Ressner and I have less than two days before the cops come down on my already sore back. Not to mention that he might go for Mae West or De Mille next."

"All right," Winning gave in. "I'll prepare the staff for your arrival. When might you be coming?"

"I'll leave this afternoon. Should get there by tonight unless I get groggy and have to stop someplace on the way. Ressner did a tune on my head. One more thing, doc. I'll need another cash payment."

"I'll have what you need when you arrive," he said.

He gave me directions on how to get to the Winning Institute. His voice had gone drier and drier and seemed about to crack when we hung up. We both had trouble, and its name was Ressner.

I pulled out some more change and dialed the Grayson number

in Plaza Del Lago. It rang and rang and rang and I waited till the baritone cowboy answered, "Grayson residence."

"Dis be Thor landscape, you know," I said as deeply as I could. "I must talk Mrs. Grayson. Joshua tree needs vork now, today or it die like dis, bang, bang, puff."

"I'm afraid she can't talk, Mr. Thor—"

"Mr. Gundersen," I corrected.

"Mr. Gundersen," he sighed with obvious exasperation reserved only for those who spoke with an accent, as if they couldn't detect sarcasm. "Mr. Grayson died just a few days ago and—"

"And the Joshua vill die, too," I said insistently.

In the background I could hear stirring and voices, and then a woman came on, voice high and nervous like Billie Burke.

"Yes, who is this?"

"Thor," I said. "Your husband Grayson vant me take care from your Joshua. Is all right I do it?"

"Yes, yes, of course, do whatever you must do, whatever Harold wanted," she bleated.

"Good, friend here vants to speak to you." I moved the phone from my ear, cleared my throat, and went to my best Toby Peters. "Mrs. Grayson, I'm an investigator for the Winning Institute. We're trying to find your former husband."

"I am very confused," she said with a very confused sob. "What are you doing with Mr. Thor, and I thought Harold was killed by some little detective."

Some little detective. O.K.

"Have you seen Jeffrey Ressner in the last week?" I demanded.

"Why yes. I told the policeman, the state policeman." Her voice quivered. "I told Jeffrey that he had to go back, but I was never very good at telling Jeffrey or Delores or anyone what they should do."

"What did Ressner want from you?"

"Money, and a call to the institute to tell them not to look for him. He was most insistent."

"Did he tell you where he was going, where he would be, where he was staying?"

"No, no."

"Do you have any idea of where he might be?"

The pause was enough to make me plunge on.

"For his sake, Mrs. Grayson. For your daughter and many innocent people. You must tell me." I was into my Dr. Christian act.

"There is a hotel in Hollywood, just off Vine. We stayed there when Delores was born and Jeffrey wanted to be an actor. He liked it there, the Los Olvidados. Something he said. I don't remember quite what made me think . . ."

"I know the place," I said. "Keep the cowboy nearby and tell Delores Toby will call her."

"Toby?" she repeated. "What about Mr. Gundersen and the Joshua?"

"He'll be out as soon as he can."

I hung up, turned around, and almost bumped into Mrs. Plaut, who was standing with a broom in her hand staring at me.

"Childish," she said.

I agreed but said nothing as I eased past her and headed down the stairs. I had a lead and might not have to head for Fresno after all.

It was a Tuesday morning. Kids were in school and the street was clear. I got in the Ford and it started with no trouble. The radio still didn't work, and I fought down the knowledge that I was doomed to endless worry about whether the car would have gas in it. I put my .38 in the glove compartment and vowed to keep a little notebook on when I filled up with gas. I knew I wouldn't do it.

There was no problem finding the Los Olvidados apartment hotel. It was a paint-peeling dump on Selma with a sagging palm out in front that looked as if it had a hangover.

The lobby was dark with a fluorescent light sputtering and crackling in the corner. The desk in the lobby was just big enough for one human to get behind, and one was there, a woman reading *Collier's* magazine and puffing on a cigarette. She was thin as a rolled-up weekday paper, and her hair was brown wire tired up in a bun.

"Can I do you for?" she said, lifting her eyes but not her head.

"Guy named Ressner registered?"

She gave me a little more attention.

"You a friend?"

"I'm more than a friend," I said and pulled out my wallet to flash the Dick Tracy badge I'd bought from my nephew Dave. She caught the glint but didn't ask to see it.

"Got no Ressner registered," she said. "What's he look like?"

"Don't know," I said. "He would have come here within the last week or so. Can you go through the names? Maybe something will ring a bell."

She lifted her bony elbow from the desk, rolled up the sleeve of her brown sweater, and put her cigarette in a tin tray. Then she pulled the gray register with a red ribbon in it and started on the names.

"Griffith, Warren, LaSconda, Benetiz, Skrinski, Grayson, Beel—"

"Grayson," I stopped her. "First name?"

"Talbott," she said. "Talbott Grayson. Hell of a name, but we get a lot of guys want to be actors and make up all kinds of crazy-ass names. Know what I mean?"

I knew this time. He had taken the names of the two men he planned to kill.

"Is he in now?" I said, putting on the friendly grin meant to calm people, but which usually had the opposite effect.

"Don't know," she said. "Don't even remember what he looks like. So many come through. He's in three D. You going up?"

"I'm going up," I said. "You want to give me a passkey?"

"I don't know," she said, cautiously hiking up her sweater to reveal knobby elbows.

"Suit yourself," I shrugged. "I can kick the door down. Or you can come with me. It might get a little pushy, so if you come, just stand back."

"I'll stay here. Got to watch the desk," she decided, handing me the key. "Bring it right back, and if you got to take him out, take him real quiet."

"Real quiet," I said.

I found the stairway, a dark, narrow gangway, and hurried up. My head was beating and I reached up to touch my bandage, fearing that it was coming off. I owed Ressner something.

Three D was at the end of a hall that smelled stale and a little wet.

I knocked, prepared to imitate the woman at the desk, the mailman, or General Wainwright. It would come to me when Ressner answered. I gripped the .38 in my pocket and knocked again. No answer. The key fit perfectly and turned easily.

"Mr. Talbott?" I squeaked, trying to do Butterfly McQueen in *Gone with the Wind*. No answer. I pulled the gun out, ready to give Ressner an airing, but it was clear that he wasn't there. There really wasn't anyplace to hide. There was one small room and a clearly visible little bathroom. It was typical prewar furnished with a bed in the corner that could look a little like a couch if the thick flower spread was put on just right, which it wasn't, a chair with a wild spring ready to goose the guest, a small table, a battered dresser, and a painting on the wall of an Oriental woman dancing with a fan in front of her nose.

The place looked empty. Drawers were open, tin wastebasket on its side. I moved to the little table, where I could see a piece of paper with some writing on it. My guess, as I took the few steps to the table, was that I'd wind up warning the woman at the desk and then come back up here to wait out the day and night in the hope that Ressner would show again, though it didn't look likely. Then I read the note:

TOO LATE, PETERS. TRY AGAIN. I'M JUST A LITTLE AHEAD OF YOU.

I put my gun in my pocket, folded the note, put it in another pocket, and went through the wastebasket. Nothing there.

I left the room and went back down the stairs.

"Not there?" hoarse-whispered the wiry woman, pointing up with her cigarette.

"No," I said, throwing her the key and hurrying across the lobby.

"What do I do if he comes back?" she continued to whisper.

"He's not coming back," I said.

I breathed deeply when I got outside, looked up at the spring sun, and felt great. I was on my way beyond Fresno.

CHAPTER 10

I stopped to get gas at a Sinclair station before I left L.A. and got a dirty look from an attendant with a Deep South accent when the Ford only took two gallons.

There was nothing much to take my mind off the pain in my scalp except the light morning traffic and my right-handed playing with the radio. Once I'd cleared town and hit 43, static hummed instead of spitting, and once, I actually got the faint murmur of a station.

A hellfire and dammit-all preacher warned me and the rest of the coast that we'd better mend our ways fast if we were going to have the moral stamina to fight off the Japanese. He pronounced stamina in three distinct syllables: sta—min—nuh. He was all I could get, so I let him keep me company, quoting from the Bible all the way to Corcoran.

I had a chicken sandwich and some war talk at the Elite Roadside Diner. The war talk was depressing, the chicken sandwich decent when washed down with the Elite's homemade orange drink.

The overtoothed guy who gave me the orange drink asked about my head, and I told him I'd got drunk and tried to ram down a door. This seemed reasonable to him.

Back on the road, the Bible belter deserted me. His voice had begun to give out, and he turned the microphone over to a woman who began to confess her sins to accompanying organ music. Her list was amazingly long and lacking in detail. After twenty miles, somewhere near Selma, the station began to fade, and my head began to crackle with static, which worried me, since I had turned off the radio. The sun was still up, bouncing out toward the ocean beyond the hills. I decided to stop for the night and tackle Winning in the morning. The problem was that I couldn't find an auto court for another ten miles, and the one I did spot was a series of gray wooden outhouses with a sign saying FREE RADIO. I pulled into the sandy driveway of Rose's Rodeo Auto Hotel, got out, stretched my legs, and went in to see if there were any vacancies. I expected to have my choice.

Rose herself, a smiling balloon of a woman, sat perched on a little stool in front of the counter.

"Room, beer, information, or gas?" she asked.

"All of them," I answered. She eased herself off the stool, waddled behind the counter, reached down, and came up with a cold Falstaff. She popped the cap and handed it to me, and I held it away while the foam eased down. It tasted fine.

"You can have cabin four," she said. "Or one, two, three, or six. Believe it or not, someone's already in five. Whatever business we get will be coming in later tonight. Going north or south?"

"Up near Clovis," I said. "Place called the Winning Institute. Heard of it?"

"Think so," said Rosie, opening her own bottle, which dripped foam over her fat wrist. "Big ugly fella of a place with teeth."

"Sounds like the fella," I said, downing some beer, which made my head throb.

"You got a relative up there?" she said.

"No, just some business."

"Something wrong with your head?" she tried, pointing at my head with her bottle in case I didn't know where my head was.

"Yeah, but nothing I need a headshrinker for. Had a little accident. I'm a salesman. Sell tongue depressors, bandages, stuff like that. Hard to get the products. Military takes most of it."

"I can imagine," said Rose, finishing her beer. "You got luggage?"

"Sure," I said, finishing off the beer and putting the empty on her desk. "I'll get it out of the trunk later, and I'll get my gas in the morning."

"Cash up front," she said, holding out the registration book, which she turned toward me. "Nothing personal."

"Good business," I said, picking up the pen and signing in as Cornel Wilde.

She looked at the signature upside down.

"You ain't Cornel Wilde," she said, stifling a burp.

"Not the actor," I chuckled. "That's my real name. Quite a burden for a tongue depressor salesman. People let me in, expecting to see a movie star. I've thought of changing my name, but what the hell, I had it first."

"I get your point. Three bucks cash plus twenty cents for the beer. You want another just to keep me company, it's free."

I pulled out my wallet, tried not to look at my dwindling cash supply, and gave her three bucks. I pulled the change out of my pocket and asked her where a good place might be for dinner.

"Not within twenty miles of here, but you're welcome to eat with me in back about eight, or go four miles down the road to Ed Don's. He runs a beanery attached to his gas station."

I gave her a soft look and she laughed.

"There's no lechery in my heart, son," she said. "I'm just an old wreck who likes to have someone to talk to on lonely nights. I'll tell you tales of the logging days up in the hills, or we can listen to the radio, or you can scat back to the cabin. No strings. Hell, I couldn't pull 'em even if I had them."

"Rosie, you got a date at eight," I said. I took the key and went through the screen door. I found cabin four with no trouble. It was right between three and five. I opened the little pop lock and went back to move my car in front of the door. I also wanted my gun and the toothbrush I'd shoved in the glove compartment.

Through the screen door I could see Rosie with a fresh bottle of Falstaff, staring at the desk as if it were a crystal ball that would tell her sad secrets.

The cabin wasn't bad, not the worst I had seen. It was clean and small. A bed with a green blanket and two pillows. A small dresser painted brown. A shower stall and a nightstand with a little radio. I turned on the radio, pulled the shades on the two windows, locked the door, and watched the road through a thin crack in the shade for whoever had followed me from the second I left Los Olvidados. He or she hadn't been too good at it, but even if they had been, it would have been a tough job. The car was big and dark and probably a Packard, but I wasn't sure. It hadn't come close enough for that.

I put the gun on my lap and kept watching. The car didn't show up for the first hour. Maybe it had lost me, but I doubted it. After "The Lone Ranger," I propped a chair in front of the door and under the knob, got undressed with the .38 within reach, and took a shower.

After the shower I checked out the window again. Another car was there, but it was a small Olds. A young couple and a kid were standing next to it, and the kid was crying loud enough so I could hear him. I got on the bed, let the radio keep playing softly, turned on my side, and closed my eyes. I slept. I think I dreamed about Cincinnati. Maybe I didn't. There was just a flicker of the dream left when I woke up. The sun was down and the room dark except for the glowing face of the radio, which informed me that it was time for Fred Waring.

I threw my pants on, shoved the gun into my jacket, turned off the radio, and went out. A few more cars but no Packard.

Rosie was waiting for me. She had changed her flour-sack dress for another flour-sack dress and put a kid's barrette in her hair.

"Thought you changed your mind," she said.

"Slept," I explained. "Hope I'm not late."

"Hell, you could have come at midnight and not been late," she chuckled and led the way beyond the counter into her back room. I followed and found a card table set up with a tablecloth and two place settings. There were two bowls on the table, both big, and a plate of dark bread. While Rosie got a pair of beers, I saw that the bowls were filled with tuna and potato salad.

"Looks great," I said and meant it.

"Dig in," she said, and we did.

"How's business tonight?" I asked innocently.

"Pretty good, still a few left. Might pick up a late one or even two before midnight. Happens sometimes."

Silence and I tried again.

"Mostly families, I suppose."

"Mostly, a few loners like you," she said, filling her fork with tuna. "Why don't you just come out with it? Who are you expecting?"

I drank some beer, let the burp come, and told her the whole tale. She kept eating through it, her eyes open wide.

"This is better than 'I Love a Mystery,'" she said. "Beats my logging stories all to hell. Tell the truth, I can't tell if you're a crazy or just the kind of guy who gets his rear in a wringer. I think you're a wringer guy."

"That's a fact." I toasted her and told her some more tales while we drank and ate. Then I listened to her tell me about logging in the old days while we had some chocolate ice cream.

"I better get some sleep," I said. "This has been great. You have my gratitude." I leaned over and gave her a kiss on the forehead. She did a three hundred-pound blush.

"Cornel Wilde," she chuckled as I walked into the front office. "I'll keep an eye out for your fella in the Packard."

"Just call me if he shows up," I said and let myself out. The screen door banged closed, sending the mosquitoes on it scurrying for a second before they returned. In the darkness, crickets chirped, and far down the road, I couldn't tell which way, a truck changed gear.

I checked my room before going in, propped the chair up, took off my clothes, and went to sleep on my side, clutching the extra pillow and letting my left hand rest on the cool steel of my .38.

Morning seemed to come in seconds. I felt great again. My gun was there. The chair was still under the knob, and my head hurt less than the day before. Everything was fine until I moved to the basin to brush my teeth and saw the window in the shower stall. It was not very big, but big enough to let someone in, and it was open. It hadn't been the night before.

There wasn't any place for someone to hide, and I was still alive.

I checked my gun. It was still loaded. I checked my pants. My wallet was missing. Twenty bucks, a driver's license, and a Dick Tracy badge. I dressed fast and paid a visit to Rosie, who sat out in front of the office her hands folded in her lap, her head back absorbing the sun.

"Rosie," I said. She opened her eyes and gave me a little smile.

"Morning," she returned, shifting her bulk in the chair, which creaked beneath her.

"I had a visitor. Someone crawled through the window and took off with my wallet. Did the guy in the Packard show up last night?"

Rosie shook her head and chins with a definite no.

"Could have come in when I went to sleep around one," she said. "In this business you sleep on and off, mostly hours when you don't expect business. Could have been a local through the nearest town, Fowler about ten miles up. Could have been another guest. We get all kinds."

"Skip it," I sighed. "You want to buy a .38 automatic?"

She said no.

"How about I leave it with you for the loan of ten bucks and I collect it on the way back with two bucks interest? I'm going to see that client I was telling you about."

"Got a better idea," Rosie said, grunting herself up from the chair. "Did some nursing back in Trenton. That's in Jersey. I'll change that bandage for you and grubstake you to ten bucks. You can drop it off on your way back through."

"You married, Rosie?" I said.

She waved for me to follow her into the office.

"Think so," she said. "Al's supposed to be cooking for a logging operation up near Portland. Left about a year, year and a half back."

"Too bad," I sighed. "I was going to propose."

"Like so much horse puddles," she chuckled, turning to sit me down. "You married?"

"Was," I said. "Not anymore. Her name was Anne."

"She dead?" asked Rose, stacking her medical cache on a nearby table.

"No. She's alive and still Anne."

"Annie, Annie was the miller's daughter," Rosie said, stepping behind me to change my bandage.

"Far she wandered from the singing water," I continued the song.

"Ain't it the way," sighed Rosie gently, tugging at my bandage. "Ain't it but the way."

Rose finished patching me, gave me ten singles from a cigar box under the front desk, and filled the Ford with gas, which added a little less than two bucks to my debt.

"Catch the bad guy," she said, waving me into the morning with a pudgy hand.

And into the north I drove, wondering why anyone would climb through a window where a man with a gun was sleeping and risk getting his face parted for a few bucks.

The rest of the drive was slow, well within the speed limit, since I didn't have a license and Rosie's ten-spot couldn't cover a speed-trap charge for driving too fast without a license.

The radio didn't help. I gave up trying to listen to a hillbilly wailing on the only station I could pick up through the static. He was singing something about losing his dream in Cal-i-for-ni-yuh and wishing he was back in Mizzuruh. Hell, I still felt good. My teeth were clean, I had a new bandage, and somewhere behind me or just up ahead was Ressner in the Packard. Sooner or later one of us would catch up with the other one. Meanwhile, I was leading him back to the Winning Institute.

Fresno came and went. I hit 41, took it to 168 and looked for the road Winning had told me to take. I almost missed it and the double billboard on the rock. I slowed down even more than the crawl I was traveling at and found the road with an enamel sign pointing the way to the Winning Institute. The road was paved, flat and narrow, not wide enough for two cars. Trees leaned down from both sides, their branches occasionally touching the top of the car and tapping a few notes.

About a mile and a half down, an arrow indicated a sharp turn. I took it and found myself in front of the metal fence of the Winning Institute. The fence was about twelve feet high, black iron with spear points at the top.

Beyond the fence about two hundred yards back was a four-story building with a two-story junior partner next to it. Both buildings were dark stone. Both had towers in the corner. It looked a little like Xanadu in *Citizen Kane*. I stayed on the road till I came to the gate, which was closed and guarded by a young blond guy in a white uniform. He was sitting in front of a little gate shack on a wooden chair, on which he leaned back so that the two front feet of it were off the ground. His back was against the fence and his arms behind his head. A newspaper rested on the ground next to him.

I leaned out of the car and said, "Hi, I'm here to see Dr. Winning."

The young guy looked over at me, shifted the gum in his mouth, and pushed forward so that all four feet of the chair rested in the dirt.

"Your name?" he said.

"Peters," I said. "Toby Peters."

"Yes," he said, getting up from the chair and pushing open the gate. "Dr. Winning said to look out for you. Drive straight on up. Park where it says 'Visitors.'"

The guy was smiling the kind of false smile you reserve for those who can't understand you and have to be tolerated. Considering the residents of the Winning Institute, it might be the attitude everybody in the place eventually adopted.

I thanked him and drove in. In the rearview mirror, I could see him push the gate closed. I drove on. The grounds on both sides were nearly flat, and in a far corner I could see someone in white pushing a mower. One man with one mower might make it a lifetime job to keep the grass of this place trim.

It was about three hundred yards to the front of the institute. Up close, I could see that both buildings were dark stone and constructed to look like castles. The porch or veranda of the larger building, where I parked in a spot with a sign marked VISITORS, threw the illusion off. It was broad, white, and wooden and looked as if it had been grafted on from a retirement hotel.

On the porch sat a quartet of men playing cards with a white-clad nurse standing over them. I got out of the car, walked across the gravel parking lot, and went up the four wooden stairs, which creaked loudly. The card players didn't look up. The nurse, from behind her glasses, gave me the same kind of tolerant smile as the guard at the gate.

"Play it or lose it," said one of the card players to another and reached over to slap at the hand of the guy across from him. The nurse turned her attention to the slapper, touched his hand, and put it back on his side of the table. I pushed through the wooden door of the building and stepped into a broad fern-filled lobby with dark wooden floors and walls papered with blue flowers and portraits of contented Winnings of the past.

A nurse was standing inside the door and off to the side. She stepped forward as if she had been waiting for me. She was about average height with brown hair and a poor complexion. Behind her stood a Negro about my height in white. He didn't give me the tolerant look. His upper body was massive, created by a comic book artist or Michelangelo.

"Mr. Peters?" she said. "I'm Nurse Grace. This is M.C. We'll take you to Dr. Winning."

I thanked them and followed her to the left. M.C. walked at my side. I wondered why I needed an armed escort. Maybe they had more reason to fear Ressner than I knew about.

We hiked down a corridor and stopped in front of an unmarked door. Nurse Grace opened it and stepped in before me. I followed her with M.C. behind me.

"Should we wash our hands before I see Dr. Winning?" I said.

"That won't be necessary," Miss Grace answered seriously.

The office was big and comfortable with a massive mahogany desk and leather desk chair behind it. There was a matching couch of leather against one wall and several not-quite-as-comfortable chairs. Behind the desk was a huge window looking across the flat grounds of the institute. No trees obstructed the view right to the fence.

I sat in one of the chairs and looked back at Nurse Grace and M.C.

"So," I tried. "Did you have a bet on the Derby?"

M.C. shook his head negatively. Nurse Grace smiled tolerantly. I touched my bandage. I'd left my hat in the car, so I couldn't play with it. Somewhere not too far away pans were clanking.

I looked at my watch without bothering to see what it said.

"I'll bet things really start jumping around here when there's a full moon," I said, turning my head to M.C., who stood to my right.

This repartee could have gone on indefinitely, but was unfortunately interrupted by a chunky guy around thirty-five, who stepped into the room through the door we had entered. He had brown unruly hair and a bushy matching moustache. His pants were dark, and he was wearing a white shirt and heavy white wool cardigan sweater with buttons.

"Sorry I'm late," he said pleasantly. "You must be Mr. . . . ."

"Peters," I said, standing and taking his hand.

"Right," he smiled, leaning back against the desk and folding his arms. "I think we can be alone now and talk a bit." He nodded at Nurse Grace, who turned and left the room with M.C. following. M.C. closed the door behind him, and I sat down again to look at the guy in the sweater.

"I'm here to see Dr. Winning," I said.

"Of course," he nodded. "We know. It's about Mr. Ressner, right?"

"That's right," I said. "You know something about Ressner?"

"Oh, quite a bit," he said. "Quite a bit. Mind if I smoke?" He pulled a pipe from his jacket and reached over for the humidor on the big desk before I could answer.

"Please, Mr. Peters, don't take any offense at this, but we have had some security problems, as you know. Could you show me some identification?"

"My wallet was stolen this morning at Rose's Rodeo Auto Court," I said. "I think I'll just wait and discuss all this with Dr. Winning. That is if he's not dead."

"Very much alive," said the guy, lighting his pipe. "Very much alive. You've met Dr. Winning?"

"Yeah," I said. "In L.A. a few days ago."

"Of course," he said, leaning back against the desk and looking at me with the tolerant smile. "Would you do me a favor? Security matter?"

"Maybe," I said, wondering is this was one of the lunatics on the loose.

"Describe Dr. Winning to me."

"Security?" I asked.

"Humor me," he said, with a grin pulling at his pipe.

"About six feet, in his fifties, blue eyes . . . That enough?"

"Yes, thanks," said the guy in the sweater, running his hand through his bushy hair and turning to pick up a pencil.

"Mr. Peters, I have some disturbing news for you," he said seriously. "And I want you to take it calmly."

"I've seen murder, mayhem, and some things you probably haven't dreamed of," I said with a delicate touch of sarcasm. "It'll take some doing to disturb me. What is it? Winning is dead? Ressner killed him last night, right?"

"No, Mr. Peters," he said, looking at me with sympathetic

brown eyes. "Dr. Winning is very much alive, as I should know, since I am Dr. Winning."

CHAPTER 11

"Well?" said Winning curiously, taking another puff on his pipe.

"Not very," I said. "Let me take a guess. That description I just gave, the Dr. Winning, that was Ressner, right?"

"With some allowances, a reasonable description of Ressner," he admitted.

My mind was clicking, but the ribbon was blank. It didn't make sense.

"How did you know I was coming? Ressner didn't call you. And why the hell did he pay me fifty bucks to . . ."

"Your sister called," Dr. Winning said.

"My sister? I don't have a sister."

"She called, or someone did, and said she was your sister. She also said your real name is Tobias Leo Pevsner." He had cheated and looked at a pad on the desk behind him.

"Right, that's my name. I changed it for business reasons. I'm a private detective."

"Of course." He moved behind the desk and sat down. "You catch criminals and protect the innocent. Just like Sam Spade."

"Something like that," I said. "Let's spend some time talking about Ressner. You want him back, don't you?"

"We want him back," said Dr. Winning. "We've informed the state police and gone through the proper channels. We wouldn't hire a private investigator. How did you hurt your head?"

The lawn mower appeared in the distance behind Winning. I tried not to watch him as he moved slowly from left to right as if he were the star of a boring movie.

"Ressner clobbered me," I explained, "just before he killed Richard Talbott, the actor."

"Ressner killed Talbott," he said evenly. "Mr. Ressner never displayed any violence in the time he spent with us."

"Well, he's much better now," I said with irritation, getting out of the chair. "He's managed to throw off his inhibitions and murder two people. You did a hell of a job with him."

"You have no identification?"

"I told you," I said with more than a little irritation. "It was stolen from me. My cash, my driver's license, and my Dick Tracy badge."

"Dick Tracy badge," he said with a tolerant pout of his lower lip.

"It's a kind of joke," I explained. "There are no private investigator badges. People like to see badges and it doesn't hurt sometimes if they think I'm a cop."

"Are you a cop?" Now he was openly taking notes.

"No, well yes, a private cop. I used to be a Glendale cop. Then I worked at Warner Brothers. My brother is a cop, an L.A. Homicide cop. You can pick up that phone and call him. Do you think I'm working some kind of con here?"

"No I don't, Mr. Pevsner," he said. "Your brother is a cop. What about your sister?"

"I don't have a sister," I said.

"What about friends?" he said, still writing. "You have any friends? I mean people who could verify your identity. Remember we have a delicate situation here. You might be a friend of Mr. Ressner."

The lawn mower was about halfway across the window and moving steadily.

"Gunther Wherthman," I said or maybe spat.

"Tell me something about him," said Winning.

"He's a midget, I mean a little person."

Winning nodded.

"He's Swiss. And there's Jeremy Butler."

"Is he a midget?" asked Winning, scratching his neck.

"No, closer to a giant. How about cutting this crap and just calling one of them or the guy I share my office with?"

"You have a partner," he said, looking up. The mower was nearing the end of the window. "Like Spade and Archer?"

"No, Shelly's a dentist."

"You are partners with a dentist."

"I didn't say he was my partner. I said we shared an office. Look, doc, we're getting nowhere here. Someone is feeding you a line, and you're taking it in. I've got a long way to go and a lot to figure out. I'll take off now. There are some people who need some help, and I can see you're not going to cooperate."

"What people?" he said, still writing. I considered ripping the pad from his desk or his nose from his face.

"Mae West and Cecil B. De Mille, to name two," I said through closed teeth.

"And, let me get this straight, you think Jeffrey Ressner is planning to hurt them, and it's your responsibility to protect them."

"You've got it straight," I said. The lawn mower was out of sight. I wanted to get up and change my angle so I could see him. He was steady and, if not sane, at least something to hold on to. "Look. You can just check your files to know about this thing with movie people. The son of a bitch went to Mae West's house four days ago dressed in drag and tried to kill me."

"Mr. Ressner tried to kill you?"

"Do you think we can carry on what's left of this conversation without you repeating everything I say? It's like listening to a dead echo."

"Sorry," he said. "A dead echo?"

I put a finger in his face and said, "I'm going."

"What happened at Mae West's house?" he went on, ignoring my farewell.

"Jeremy saved my damned life," I said.

"Jeremy's the midget," he said.

"No, the giant. That's it. I'm going. If I find Ressner, I'm turning him over to the cops. I think I've had it over my head with the Winning Institute."

"One last thing," Winning said still ignoring my anger. "Mr. Pevsner, your sister has asked us to keep you here for observation for a few days, possibly longer. She's told us that you've had sessions like this before and can be self-destructive. Mr. Pevsner, we found the gun in your car."

"It's registered," I said. "Just put it back, you son of a bitch. It's my property. I don't have much property, but what I've got, I like to protect."

"Your sister says that in fact you have quite a bit of property back in Arizona." Winning rose and looked at me. "Her check to us this morning was quite generous. Now why would a sister you don't have give us a generous check?"

I drew in my breath for one last try before I threw Dr. Winning's tolerant body through the window.

"I've been set up," I said. "Ressner pretended to be you, got me up here, took my wallet, paid someone to call saying she was my sister."

"Why would Mr. Ressner do that?" Winning said reasonably,

putting his pipe down in a neat wooden ashtray.

"To get me out of the way while he goes for Mae West and De Mille. Because he doesn't like me and thinks he has a score to settle. Because he is a nut, something you are supposed to know something about."

Winning wrote something and put the pad down.

"Nope," he said sadly, "Where would Jeffrey Ressner get the kind of money that came here this morning? And your story. Put yourself in my position, Mr. Pevsner."

"Peters," I corrected, making a fist.

"Peters," he said with a smile. "If there is some kind of plot by Ressner, we'll find out about it. Why not just cooperate with us for a day or so? You can have a nice rest here, all paid for. We'll check your story, your brother, your friends."

Our eyes met, and I could tell that I was being humored. I tried to think of a way of breaking through that tolerance, and then I gave up.

"You know what I think I'll do?" I said.

"No, what?"

"I think I'll just walk out of here quietly if I can, but if I can't I'll bounce you off the wall."

Winning wasn't fazed.

"Like a dead echo?" he said and put his hand under the desk. I could hear a buzzing sound in the hall and realized he had hit a hidden button.

I turned to the door as M.C. stroke in with Nurse Grace a pace behind him.

"Mr. Pevsner will be staying with us for at least a day or so," said Winning, tapping his notepad.

"Step out of the way, M.C.," I said, holding out my arm.

"No trouble," he said, blocking the doorway.

"I think we're a little late for that," I said, easing to the right with the idea of a fast dash past M.C. and a wild end run over Nurse Grace.

"Maybe so," he said. Everybody in the damn place was reasonable.

"I'm going now," I said, taking a step forward.

M.C.'s head shook a soft no. I turned to Dr. Winning, who watched with sad paternal eyes. I was one of his now.

I made my move and threw my shoulder at M.C. He side-stepped and grabbed for my arm. He missed. I pushed Nurse Grace and headed down the hall. I got no more than ten feet before M.C. caught me around the waist and lifted me in the air. I felt like a football about to take part in a brutal punt return.

"Go easy, my man," he said in my ear.

I threw an elbow at his head and felt it connect. My elbow hurt but he didn't loosen up. Instead he sat me on the ground. I could hear footsteps coming up behind us and caught a glimpse of Nurse Grace's white shoes.

"You need some help?" she said.

"Just put him out," said M.C. still softly, as if he wanted this over with so he could get on to more important things. He grabbed my right wrist and clamped it tight. Nurse Grace was on her knees, and I could see something in her right hand, a hypodermic needle.

"I've been vaccinated," I said, struggling to get free.

"Not for this trip," said M.C., and the needle went into my forearm.

I think Koko tried to stop them. At least he was there almost instantly and happier than ever before. He was beautifully clear and, for the first time, in color. I wanted to open my eyes and tell M.C. and Nurse Grace that Koko had appeared in color, but I couldn't. Koko took my hand and led me to the inkwell. I had things to do, people to save, but he was not to be denied. We balanced at the end of the inkwell, and just before we plunged in, I could see a pen descending on us. The pen looked suspiciously like a needle.

When I awoke, I had the feeling that just seconds had passed. I was lying on a bed. To my left was another bed. Beyond that bed was a wall with a small, barred window leading to the night. A circular fluorescent light fixture in the low ceiling revealed white walls. On the other bed, a powerful-looking man with brownish-yellow hair reclined comfortably in bright green and red pajamas and read a book. It was *Frenchman's Creek* by Du Maurier.

We looked at each other for a few moments before I turned my back and closed my eyes. But I couldn't sleep and knew it. If anything, I had a headache from too much drugged sleep. When I was feeling under the blanket to find out what I was wearing (it turned out to be a pair of hospital gray pajamas), I realized that since I was a potential psychotic, my roommate must also be a mental patient. I might be unwise to turn my back on him. In turning quickly to face the man in the bright green and red pajamas, I forgot about the stitches in my head.

"You got a headache?" the man said. "You want a drink?" He leaned forward, blinking.

"No. No thanks."

"Mind if I exercise?" He put his book aside and stood next to me between the beds.

"No."

The man suddenly disappeared, and it took me a few seconds to realize that he had dropped to the floor. Leaning dizzily over, I found him sitting crosslegged, teeth clenched, and red-faced. He grunted slightly and turned redder. As the red began to turn to white, he relaxed and turned on his stomach. It seemed as if he had gone to sleep, but instead he threw his arms back and lifted his legs from the floor so that he was carefully balanced on his stomach and looking in vacant agony at the wall ahead of him. Again he failed to make any impression on the wall except for fingerprints, which joined the pattern of other, older fingerprints at approximately the same point.

"You were wondering why I waited till you woke up to do my exercises, weren't you?"

"No," I said, trying to shake the drug dryness from my tongue and brain.

"Truth is I like an audience. I used to feel guilty about that." He dabbed his perspiring face with the corner of his bright pajamas. "Used to find myself exercising whenever company came over, and my wife would say I was just showing off. I never thought I was showing off. Just did it when the mood took me and didn't stop to analyze it. The hell with her. I said it then and I say it now."

We looked at each other in silence for a minute or longer.

"My name is Sklodovich, Ivan Sklodovich," he said, extending a hand, which I shifted to meet with my unsteady grasp. "Don't worry, I won't squeeze. I don't believe in tests of strength on a first meeting. It creates a competitive tension that's hard to overcome. You know what I mean?"

"Yes. My name is Peters, Toby Peters."

"Nice to meet you. Listen, Toby. They call me Cortland around here. The staff, I mean. I don't like it, but live and let live. It doesn't cost me anything to be called Cortland, does it?"

"No."

"You see my father was a welder in Russia and when he came to America he invented a new welding process, Slig. A big tycoon was what my old man wanted to be, so he changed his name to Cortland. But it didn't help. Nobody wanted Slig welding, and nobody wanted a roly-poly bearded Russian with a name like Cortland. They thought he was a Bolshevik spy or something. For twenty years my family has hidden the solid, black-bread name of Sklodovich behind the chewing-gum name of Cortland. But no more. I am Ivan Sklodovich. Peters. Are you the Peters who paints murals in sewers?"

"No, I'm a detective."

"A defective?"

"Detective. A private eye."

"Oh. I couldn't figure out what the hell a defective was. This is a mental hospital, you know?"

"Yes, I know," I said and told him my story in condensed form, during which he blinked frequently and ate an orange pulled from under his pillow after first offering it to me.

When I mentioned Ressner, Cortland-who-would-be-Sklodovich paused in his citrus munching and nodded wisely.

"I know Ressner," said Cortland, after I had finished telling him of how I became a prisoner in Winning. "I used to work in an office, sold carbon paper, Whitney Carbon Paper, the carbon paper that leaves a clean impression on the paper and no smudges on your hand. You've heard of them? From salesman, trudging from stationery shop to drugstore to school supply store, I was promoted to North San Diego regional director of sales with a near-sighted secretary and my own office in an old building with windows that looked like rejects from the Union Station bathroom. My secretary, Phyllis, took off her glasses one day, and I fell in love and married her. Carbon paper sales rose in North San Diego, and I moved up to assistant Midwest sectional division manager in charge of complaints. This brought me to L.A., where Phyllis learned to play bridge, and sales boomed."

At this point I must have made a face, for Sklodovich said: "Be patient. I'll get to Ressner."

"Sorry," I said.

"Now that I think about it, I don't really know what I did those four years in the main office. Then sales fell. Who knows why? Carbon sales depend upon little competition and a triplicate society. In any case, bills mounted, my commission dropped, Phyllis had an abortion, skinny old John Whitney Lickter began to get on me, and I began to worry seriously about Hitler. But Lickter was the worst of all because I had to face his shriveled, frowning face every day with excuses. It got to the point where I couldn't stand to hear his 'Is that your total and complete report, Mr. Cortland? It leaves much to be desired.' If any single thing drove me mad, it was that statement from him each morning while he sipped tea from a mug marked J.W.L. and played with the perpetual mole on his chin, the old fart. You don't mind if I use a bit of profanity to color my speech, do you?"

"Not at all."

"We do have to make some allowances for each other. After all we are mentally unwell. You don't mind if I refer to our mental problem, do you?"

"I haven't got any mental problem. They've made a mistake, I told you." I tried to sit up and swallow, but the will was not enough. Ressner could be merrily hacking away at Mae West while I pretended to listen to this ranting maniac.

"Perhaps," said Sklodovich, lying back on his bed. "It wouldn't be the first time and it wouldn't be the last. I hope you don't mind the homilies. Do you? Actually I shouldn't spend so much time apologizing. That was one of my problems. Always apologizing to my wife, to Lickter, to stationery store owners."

"You were going to tell me about Ressner."

"Oh yes. Well, one morning after I had lost my bus transfer and fought with the driver over changing a five-dollar bill, old Lickter called me into his office to grumble and complain about the lack of sales. You wouldn't think to look at me, but I used to be a real worm; that's a fact. I was home and office doormat. I handed old Lickter my report as usual and he read it grim-faced, glancing up at me through the smoke of his cigar or the steam of his tea; either of the two was constantly at his mouth. 'Is that your total and complete report, Mr. Cortland? It leaves much to be desired.' Instead of nodding in fear for my fragile reputation as I had previously, I grabbed the old man, took his damned cigar, tied him with the cord from his draw drapes, and dangled him out of the window fifteen stories above the sidewalk. He was too frightened to say much at first, but as soon as I tied one end of the cord to his desk I heard him screaming to the sunny sky. 'The situation does leave a great deal to be desired, doesn't it, Mr. Lickter?' I called out the window and peered over to see a crowd gathering. 'Cut the rope, man,' someone shouted. 'No, no,' said another guy, 'wait till I get my camera.' Mr. Seymour, my immediate superior, chief Midwest sectional division manager in charge of erasers, came into the office about five minutes later with a smile on his false and lecherous face. 'What's going on here, Craig? Some kind of misunderstanding with Mr. Lickter? Can I help in any way?' 'I hung him out the window, you queer bastard,' I said, tweaking his effeminate nose. I pulled him by the nose to the window and shouted down to the waiting crowd, 'Mr. Seymour here is a queer.' 'Wha' he say?' I heard a woman shout. 'He says Seymour is a fairy,' said another voice. 'Which one's Seymour?' 'This one,' I shouted. 'Atta boy, Mac, toss him down here.' Seymour, nostrils stopped, pleaded 'led mbe go, please,' 'Mr. Lickter, you knew Mr. Seymour here was a queer, didn't you?' 'Let me up, Mr. Cortland, I promise I'll pay you anything,' shouted Lickter, whose upsidedown face was quite red. I shoved Seymour, the corrupter of office boys, into the large closet behind the huge desk. Next a cop came up and talked to me through the door, though the door wasn't locked. 'This is Sergeant Derk, Cortland. What have you done with Seymour?' 'He's in the closet,' I said, 'but why you should care is beyond me.' 'Now,' said Sergeant Derk slowly, 'I want you to listen to me. Cutting that rope isn't going to solve any problems,' Do you think this whole thing sounds Freudian? I mean their fear that I might cut the imaginary umbilical cord that bound me to his authority."

"It does sound a little Freudian," I said, feeling a little reasonable fear of the orange-eating, talkative lunatic in the next bed.

"I didn't even think about cutting the cord until he brought it up. But I didn't answer Sergeant Derk, who went away after a few seconds. 'Is there anything to be desired out there?' I asked Mr. Lickter. He said nothing, and I noticed that the fire department had spread a net below the window and was busily at work on an additional net a few stories below. I helped Lickter up, and the now-massive crowd groaned. 'Don't worry,' I shouted. 'He'll be right back.' 'Please Cortland,' he sputtered, seated upright on the window ledge. 'I'll make you a partner,' 'Be realistic,' I said, turning him upside down again when the normal paste color had returned. The crowd cheered. 'How can you make me a partner? You know as well as I do that if I let you in, I'll be thrown in jail and fired. You'd have to be crazy to make me a partner.' Toby—do you mind if I call you Toby?"

"Not at all."

"Next they sent a priest up to talk to me even though I'm not a Catholic. Why is it they always send a priest even though most people are not Catholics?"

Before I could answer he continued talking.

"The priest was a pleasant, chubby guy who looked scared to death but determined, so I let him in. 'This is not the way, Craig. You can gain nothing from this. Let them go, and I'll do what I can to help you.' 'You don't even know me,' I said. 'I don't have to know you, but I can see that you are a man who respects the laws of God.' 'I respect neither God, man, nor the Internal Revenue Service, father.' 'That is blasphemy, young man,' he said gently. 'Yes,' I replied, wishing they had sent a more capable priest. But I'm sure they sent what they had on hand. 'I'll have to insist that you let that man in,' said the priest. There was no choice for me."

"You let him up?"

"No, I tied up the priest with the cord from the other drape, and he joined Lickter out the window. I'm not boring you, am I?"

"No."

"Good. Well they sent Phyllis, but I wouldn't let her in. There was no more drape cord, and I already had someone in the closet. She cried for a while and went away. You're wondering about Ressner, aren't you?"

"Yes," I said.

"The phone had been ringing the moment I lowered the priest out the window and heard the faraway voices below: 'It's a priest.' 'God no.' 'He gonna drop a priest?' 'That'd be something.' 'Oh, they'll fall in the net.' 'Father,' I called. 'That is Mr. Lickter.' 'Courage,' said the priest. 'That's the spirit, father,' I shouted before answering the phone."

Sklodovich reached under his pillow for a fresh orange.

"Then a red-faced old cop with a gun in his hand came outside the door and fired a bullet in the air. 'Come out of there with your hands on your head or I'll come in there and shoot you in the balls,' he shouted indiscreetly. I was wondering why no one had thought of doing this earlier."

"What did you do?"

"What did I do? For Chrissake I opened the door and let him in. I'm crazy, but I'm not stupid. I could tell that little son of a bitch meant business. I found out later he got a medal and they fired him for risking all those lives. A few months afterward I read in the paper that he was suspected of working for the syndicate."

"Ressner?" I reminded him.

M.C. walked in as Sklodovich was about to speak again. He motioned to me to follow him, and I looked at Sklodovich, who was smiling at M.C.

"When are we going to arm-wrestle, M.C.? You know you're going to give in eventually. Now is as good a time as any."

M.C. paid no attention to Cortland's question as I rose on weak knees, put on a pair of slippers that I found next to the bed, and started out of the room.

"Now I ask you, Toby. How can a man refuse a challenge like that and retain his dignity? See you later."

M.C. grasped my arm and led me down a corridor of doors, past a large alcove with old couches and magazines, and by a glass-enclosed desk across from two elevators. At the desk sat two nurses, a short, young pretty one and an old thin one with a thin mouth that hardly moved as she spoke to the young girl. A tall, barrel-chested, hairy-armed man with short hair stood behind them with his arms folded. He was dressed in the same white uniform that M.C. wore, and the two men exchanged understanding glances. We stopped before the elevators, and I watched the lights go on 1-2-3-4. M.C. pressed the black button with the faded white 4 on it and concentrated on the wall as we rose.

I had decided that I would have to go along and look for a chance to get away. The fourth-floor lobby contained an enclosed desk (PLEASE DO NOT FEED THE NURSES), an alcove of empty chairs, a desk and a corridor of rooms. A young doctor stood in the hall, speaking to an even younger nurse. They looked at me as we passed. At the end of the hall we stopped at a door that looked like the others. M.C. opened it, motioned me in, and closed the door, leaving me alone to face two men seated at a table in a small, bare room with a cheap Degas reproduction tilted on the wall.

One man, the one with a small pointed white beard and a bald head popping through a fringe of gray hair, smiled and pointed with the stem of his pipe at an empty chair. I sat in it. The other man, a young Arabian-looking serious type with thick black hair, split his attention between me and the older man, with whom he shared an ashtray for their quite similar pipes.

The older doctor (Thomas Mitchell with an earache) leaned back and flipped through a chart in front of him, his underlip curled over his upper and his eyebrows up as if straining to let in maximum light.

"My name is Dr. Vaderg—" and his voice cracked and went squeaky. Coughing, Dr. Vaderg—reached for a glass of water while his dark companion looked helplessly about, not knowing what to do. I pretended not to notice, but the incident obviously had shattered a carefully prepared scene. The old doctor drank, recovered, smiled slightly, and cleared his throat. I joined him in a thin, careful smile.

"My name is Dr. Vadergreff. My colleague is Dr. Randipur." Dr. Randipur nodded.

"Your name, it is Toby Peters?" said Dr. Randipur, looking down at a pad of paper.

"Yes." Such an answer, I thought, must be safe.

"Mr. Toby Peters. May I ask of you why is it you think you may now be here?" said Randipur, after a glance from Vadergreff, who nodded in approval at the question.

"A mistake."

"Dr. Winning"—smiled old baldy—"seldom makes mistakes. As a matter of fact, I can't recall him ever making a diagnostic error. He may have some minor disagreements with some of us on treatment procedures, but after all, this is a research institute and unusual cases require unusual treatment. No, I'm afraid we'll have to look elsewhere for an explanation." Dr. Radipur jotted down this pithy statement.

With a blank, expressionless gaze I hoped would pass for sincere attention, I fixed upon Dr. Vadergreff's ample nose. Somehow I had given the impression that Dr. Winning had been accused of error. Since this concept was impossible for the old man, I tried to make it seem as if I had made the mistake as a result of my ignorance about Dr. Winning's infallibility.

"Now, Mr. Peters," Vadergreff continued through the clenched teeth, which held his pipe, "how do you account for your behavior this morning? It seems you threatened Dr. Winning and became violent. If this report is right, you had to be subdued."

My moment had come. I told them the whole story.

When I finished, the two doctors leaned over for a whispered consultation. The old man's eyebrows pointed up as he listened.

"We, Dr. Randipur and I, feel that you have had a difficult day, and perhaps it would be better to let you get some rest. Be assured that we are neither quacks nor fools. We are trained physicians trying to help you. Please give us the benefit of any doubts you may have and accept the help we offer."

Vadergreff rose, and I was surprised to see how short he was. Randipur and I also rose. Vadergreff pushed a white button on the desk with his left hand. The two doctors stood frozen-smiled, waiting for someone to come and remove me so that they could relax and discuss my case, old mentor to eager pupil.

"Dr. Vadergreff."

"Yes."

"I would like to see Dr. Winning again."

"Sorry, Dr. Winning has left for the night, but I'll tell him tomorrow you want to see him. I believe he has a speaking engagement in Los Angeles, however, and won't be back here until Friday. Can Dr. Randipur or I help you?"

"Tomorrow may be too late. We've got two murders. There could be two more in the next few days. Are you two in there? Do you understand what I've been saying?"

The door opened, and M.C. moved quickly to take my arm and guide me out.

"Do you think there's something wrong with me?"

He looked at me for a few seconds before shrugging noncommittally. Three minutes later I could hear him locking the door behind me when I stepped into my room.

Sklodovich was leaning forward with the palms of both hands against the wall in a vain attempt to push it over.

"How'd it go?" he asked, pushing himself from the wall and wrapping a towel around his neck.

"Fine."

"They still think you're nuts, huh?"

"Yes."

"You don't feel like talking? I know how you feel. Sure you wouldn't like to punch me in the stomach? It would be a great opportunity to release repressed hostility, and I'd never feel it."

"Goodnight," I said, closed my eyes and slept.

"Goodnight."

*   *   *

Maybe it was an hour, maybe it was two. Someone was shaking me. I opened my eyes to darkness and hoped it was Phil, Jeremy, or even Gunther or Mrs. Plaut. I'd even settle for Shelly.

It was Sklodovich.

"Get up," he whispered. "I've got a meeting arranged with Dealer."

"Great," I whispered back. "We'll talk in the morning."

I closed my eyes.

"Are you getting up?"

"No."

His hand grabbed my stomach, and for a second I thought he was going to kill me, but I soon realized that he was tickling me.

"Cu—cu—cut it out," I chuckled.

"Are you getting up?"

"No." I tried to curl into a ball, but he straightened my legs with no difficulty. I tried to roll off the bed as nausea welled, but he held me with one powerful, hairy arm and continued to tickle while I grew sore from laughter.

"O.K.," I pleaded. "O.K."

He stopped. A few more guffaws ached my head, but I stood up.

"You want to get out of here, or you want to get out of here?" he asked reasonably. "Dealer can get you out. He got Ressner out."

"He got Ressner out?"

I forced myself up and looked at Sklodovich. The pattern of bars cast by moonlight through the window made him look as mad as he surely was.

"Dealer's been in this place for years, longer than anybody. Psychiatry staff is meeting now. They meet every night about now. It'll be at least an hour before they break up and anyone could think of coming here to check us. Let's move. See if the door's locked."

I put on the robe he handed me and took the slippers he shoved into my hand. Standing wasn't easy, but I did it.

I shuffled to the door and tried it. It was locked.

Sklodovich put his ear to the door, listened for a moment, and rapped twice on the wall to the left. Someone on the other side returned the two raps and Sklodovich smiled.

"What's Dealer's problem?" Sklodovich asked.

"I don't know. I never even heard of him till you mentioned him."

"I meant that you should ask me what his problem is. I was prompting you," said Sklodovich, taking a small wire from the heel of his right slipper and carefully placing it in the lock.

"O.K. What's his problem?"

"He's a prisoner. Sometimes he's in a German prison camp or concentration camp and he's a Jew or a British officer. Sometimes he's in a Japanese labor compound and he's an American sergeant. Or he's a counterrevolutionary in a Siberian work gang. Sometimes he's very specific. Once he was the man in the iron mask. Another time he was Edmund Dantes in the Château d'If."

"He sounds like a big help."

"I think so too. Come on."

The small wire made a clicking sound in the door, which opened slightly. Sklodovich peeped out and scanned the floor in both directions before darting into the room next door, from which he had received the two answering raps. I followed, robe wrapped tightly, slippers flopping.

Sklodovich closed the door, and we faced a small, birdlike man with wild gray hair and huge saucer eyes, which bulged in a looked of constant surprise. The white-gowned creature eyed me for several seconds, then reached up, pulled Sklodovich's head down, and whispered in a loud voice:

"A guy came wit you."

"I know," Sklodovich replied in the same stage whisper. "He's with me."

"You are sure?"

"Yes. Are you?"

"Me? Me? Me?" said the bird, his great eyes darting about in astonishment. "What did you ask me?"

"He's with me."

"Good." He looked in triumph at me and scratched his head. A few wisps of hair rose ridiculously. "Just want to be sure, you know. Tell me," he whispered again, pulling Sklodovich's sleeve into a crinkly mess, "are they still out there?"

"No. Look out there for yourself."

"Me? Me? Me? Look out there? No tank you, buster. Not me. What you think I am?" He looked at me for an answer, but I could supply none, since I didn't think anything about him other than he was a genuine madman.

"Toby and I have got to see Dealer."

"Toby?"

"This is Toby. He came in with me."

"I see," said the man sagely. "Come wit me." He turned into the room which looked exactly like our own except for a closet where we had a blank wall. One bed was neatly made. In the other, a large bulge under a crazy-quilt blanket was shivering with fear, illness, or shock. The bird opened the closet door.

"They maybe ain't there now," he mumbled, moving boxes from the closet floor to one side, "but open that door and they'll be there so fast, it'll make you pee-pee in you pants I tell ya."

Sklodovich nodded, reached down, and removed a plasterboard panel from the back of the closet wall. Beyond the panel I could see a tile floor. Sklodovich stepped through the hole and motioned me to follow. I stepped into a large bathroom, and the bird replaced the plasterboard and whispered: "You tink I don't know they out there you got anudder tink?"

"Who does he think is outside the door?"

"I don't know," said Sklodovich. "He'd rather not say."

Sklodovich listened at the door for a second, then strode to the nearest stall to the accompaniment of swirling water in the line of automatic constantly flushing cleanser-needful urinals.

I followed.

Inside the stall, above the toilet, was a small, metal door painted battleship gray. Sklodovich pulled it open.

"Up the pipe," he whispered, pointing his finger up the dark shaft beyond the door.

At first I thought he was muttering a dark-purpled curse against pipes and tubular constructions. After all, he was, by confession and choice, a lunatic. Headfirst, Sklodovich disappeared through the hole.

"Close the door behind you," his voice echoed seconds after his slippered toes vanished.

Reaching into the darkness, I felt a moist water pipe and began to pull myself painfully into the darkness, pausing to close the metal door behind me.

There I balanced, clinging to a wet pipe with one hand and both legs while with my other hand I attempted to close a heavy metal door that had no handle on the inside, nothing but a protruding bolt, which I struggled to grasp with unprotected fingers.

Plunged in darkness, my fear increased. How many floors below me did this blackness fall? If my grip and the surrounding wall in the narrow tunnel failed me, would I zip down into a limbo like razor blades into those shafts in hotel bathrooms? And up? What was up above me except the retreating sound of Sklodovich's breathing?

Using the wall, a jagged mass of rough bricks, and piping, I managed to follow within hearing distance of my guide. I skinned my right arm on an unidentified outcropping, and my wet hands kept slipping, but I rested without too much difficulty by holding the pipe and letting my rear end rest against a smooth section of wall. I continued like this in the timelessness of darkness for a period of between two minutes and four hours.

My back ached, but I climbed upward. My pajama bottoms slipped, but I grappled upward. My palms blistered, but I moved onward. My foot found an exceptionally good hold on a protruding brick and I pushed myself forward and found a long, thin face gazing at me. The face included a mouth that hung stupidly open, inches from me. A gray stubble of beard surrounded the open mouth, which revealed a pitted and not very pleasant tongue. I almost let go.

Sklodovich's face replaced the one that had startled me.

"Where have you been, Toby? I thought you changed your mind. Hell, I guess there aren't many men who can make it up the shaftway as quickly as I can. Dynamic tension does it. With nothing but dynamic tension Charles Atlas got strong enough to pull railroad cars. Think of that. Railroad cars. A man who can pull railroad cars doesn't get sand kicked in his face at the beach, or anywhere else. You know Atlas volunteered to beef up old Gandhi in India?"

"Can I come in? My feet are slipping."

"Sure. I'm sorry," said Sklodovich, helping me through the hole, which turned out to be another shaftway entrance in another washroom like the one we had left. I stepped over the toilet and leaned against the wall to catch my breath.

A man with his mouth open stood there with his pajamas at his feet, watching us. He was very tall and thin and leaned forward with rounded shoulders. His grayish skin made him look like a wilted stalk of celery. He had obviously been interrupted while seated.

"Let's go," said Sklodovich, walking to the door.

"Does he know what we're doing here?" I asked.

"He?"

"This man," I said, nodding toward the celery-man, whose look of astonishment was firmly frozen on his face.

"I suppose not. Why?"

"Why? I think we scared the hell out of him."

"You think so," asked Sklodovich seriously. "Did we scare the hell out of you, fella?"

The man shook his head wildly.

"See we didn't scare him. You can have your pot back, mister. Now let's go. If you see anybody in the hall, walk as if you belong here."

Without knowing how one walks when one belongs on a particular floor of a nut house, I followed Sklodovich into the hall, leaving the bewildered man to make his own peace with reality.

There were patients in the hall, but they paid no attention as we went down a corridor like the one on our own floor. A nurse passed, paused, and turned to me. Sklodovich kept walking, but I stopped when I felt her arm on my sleeve.

"Don't you think you should take off that robe and get a clean one?" she asked. "You look as if you've been crawling down a greased pole."

"I don't know how it got so dirty. Must have fallen. I'll change it right away."

"See that you do."

She walked away to talk to another patient, and I hurried after Sklodovich, whom I found down a short corridor. He stopped in front of a window overlooking an enclosed courtyard. The window was hidden from the main corridor by a pillar. Sklodovich opened the window and gently pushed two of the bars covering it out of the way. He slid through and motioned for me to follow. I did.

Sklodovich closed the window and pushed the bars back in place. It was only then that I noticed we were standing on a narrow ledge four floors above the ground, a ledge that tilted slightly downward. A thin rain was falling, but Sklodovich began shuffling along the ledge, and I followed. After two steps on the wet ledge, I decided to climb through the next window and turn myself in for the safety of my room. We inched our way along the ledge, but came to no window. Sklodovich stopped.

I could see him from the corner of my eye. My back was tight against the wall and my head as far back as I could pull it without cracking the stitching open. Sklodovich reached up to an old rainspout, pulled himself up with one hand, and disappeared.

With trembling hand and rain-moistened body I shuffled over, reached for the rainspout, and tried to lift myself, but my foot slipped. "Not in my pajamas," I screamed, picturing myself plunging downward.

Sklodovich reached over and grabbed my wrist, but my legs gave way and I glanced down to watch my slippers plunge, bounce against the wall, and melt into the rain. Twisting, I tried to regain a foothold. My robe flapped in my eyes, and I had the uncomfortable feeling that my pajama bottoms had slipped and I was, like the celery-man in the washroom exposed from the waist down.

Sklodovich lifted me easily over the top without bouncing me against the rainspout. I found myself on the roof of the hospital, lying on a pebbled asphalt surface and feeling like a mop left out overnight in the rain.

"I'll carry you the rest of the way if you like," Sklodovich offered.

"No thanks," said I, rising amid the sparse jungle of chimneys and parapets. "I'll make it."

Limping barefoot on the pebbles, I followed Sklodovich behind a protuberance of concrete and found us facing a green door. Sklodovich put his ear to the door and opened it gently.

"It opens from the outside but not the inside," he whispered.

"I see," I panted, but I did not see at all.

"Put these on," Sklodovich ordered as we stepped through the door. He handed me a pair of sunglasses, which I put on and which did not help at all in navigating the narrow stairway down which we tiptoed.

"If anyone asks you, we're on our way to Dr. Keaky for a heat treatment," he said, putting on a pair of sunglasses.

"What if they ask us why we're wet?"

"We just took showers."

"But our robes and pajamas are wet"

"I know that."

"I know that you know it," I whispered. "But what do we tell someone if they ask why our clothes are wet?"

"We fell in the pool."

"Is there a pool?"

"I don't know," said Sklodovich as we hurried down a dozen stairs in sticky flight. "But no one will question it. We're supposed to be mentally unstable, remember?"

"What else is there to remember around here?"

We reached another door and Sklodovich turned to me.

"Remember, we're on our way to Dr. Keaky for a —"

"Heat treatment."

"Right."

Dripping, we stepped into another hospital alcove. The sunglasses made everything seem warm and sweaty, which it was.

"Wait behind the door," he said. "Dealer is somewhere on this floor, but I'm not sure of the room. It'll just take me a minute."

Before I could protest, he plunged his hands into his pockets and stepped into the hallway, whistling more conspicuously than I thought safe.

Alone, I noticed a single door in the alcove where I was standing. The door was slightly open, and glancing at it, I was sure it was opening an almost infinitesimal fraction each second. Just as I was about to step back behind the safety of my own door, the door swung open and a short, dark man who looked like an Italian bus driver stepped out. One hand was calmly resting in the pocket of a black silk robe. The other hand, his left I believe, held a pistol pointed at my stomach.

CHAPTER 12

"You will please step into this room," said the dark-haired man quietly.

"I'm on my way to Dr. Keaky for a heat treatment."

"Nonsense. There is no Dr. Keaky. Please step into this room with no more trouble." He looked toward the hallway, where Sklodovich had disappeared, and motioned with his gun toward the door before which he was standing. I stepped in, leaving moist footprints on the tile floor.

He followed and closed the door. The room was much like the one that my dubious friend and I occupied, except that it seemed much more permanent and held only one bed in the corner. There was a simple, unpainted wood table and chair, a reproduction of a van Gogh sunflower on one wall, and a big trunk in another corner.

"You will sit on the chair, and I will sit on the bed, where it will be quite impossible for you to make a move toward me and live. Very good. You did not know that I could open the door, did you? Of course not. You never see the obvious. In many ways you are clever, but in the end, your overconfidence will trip you up."

"You've got me confused with someone else. To be frank, I'm a patient, like you. My name is Peters. I'm just looking for someone on this floor named Dealer and—"

"Take off your sunglasses, please."

I took them off and found the man not so dark as I had thought, but the pistol was much larger than I had feared.

"We might be able to arrange some kind of deal," he said.

"A deal?"

"Perhaps. Remember, I can always kill you, push you outside, and close the door. The others do not know that I've got this gun nor that I can open the door. Do not move."

"I'm not moving."

"As I was saying," he continued, "no one would suspect me."

"Who would they suspect?"

He laughed.

"You don't trust each other. You fight. I've heard you at night when you think I'm sleeping. You have an enemy here, I'm sure. You all have. They'll blame him. So you see you have no choice but to help me. You understand?" He waved the gun.

"You're making a—"

"Do you understand?" he repeated in a quiet voice, raising the gun.

"Yes."

"Good. First we will change clothes. You take yours off first."

"My clothes are wet," I protested. "Beside they won't fit you and what good would they do? They're not much different from your own."

"Very clever," said the man with sincere admiration. "Very

clever indeed. For that I give you credit. I advise you not to move another step."

"I didn't move."

"Very good. I should hate to have to shoot you before you've served my purpose. Now we must hurry."

"What the hell is this all about?"

"You persist in this charade, do you?" he said. "I begin to think that you are not so smart. But perhaps you are simply stalling for time. Are you expecting someone?" He moved quickly to the door, looked out, closed it, and walked over to me.

"Mr . . ."

"Peters."

"Peters, or whatever your name is, you will walk out of this room in front of me and lead me out of here as if you were taking me someplace. You understand? My gun will not be visible, but it will be in my pocket trained on your abdomen. It has a hair trigger. Do you know anything about guns?"

"I know about guns," I said.

"I hope you know enough to determine that this is a real gun." He held it up cautiously and I could see it was a .45.

"It's real," I said.

"I'm glad you see that."

"You're making a hell of a mistake. We'll get halfway down the hall and they'll grab both of us. You don't seem to understand that I'm a patient too."

"You would like me to believe that. I know you have been planted here. I can always spot you. Now we have wasted enough time. Would you like a drink before we start to give you a little brace and tighten up your nerves? I knew when the shoe was on the other foot, you'd be cowards."

"I have no shoes."

"Pleading will accomplish nothing. Now if you will just do as you are told, you may get through this alive. We will walk slowly, speaking to no one. We will pass the nurse station near the elevators, step into the elevators, and go down to the basement."

"But you have no clothes."

He smiled shyly, reached under his bed, and pulled out a small, brown paper bag neatly tied with string.

"My clothes are in here. Nothing fancy, but they will suffice. You think all this will help you to track me down later, but it won't. I have friends. Now let's go. Remember that I will not hesitate to use this gun. I have nothing to lose. If you stop me this time, I'm sure you will never give me another opportunity to escape, and I'll be lucky to live through the day."

"But—"

"One more word and I'm afraid I'll have to shoot. I'm not sure how effective this silencer is, but if I have to try it, I will."

I walked to the door.

"You're making a mistake."

"Perhaps," said the little man, who was now at the door. "It won't be the first time, and let's hope for both of our sakes that it will not be the last either. I regret we no longer have time for a last drink of Old Sweat Sox. Be good enough to step into the hall."

The man, gun carefully pointed at me, opened the door to reveal Sklodovich, hand raised to knock.

"Got the corridors confused," said Sklodovich, walking in and sitting on the chair. "Well, does he know anything?"

I was not sure to whom the question was addressed, but it seemed senseless in either case and was answered with silence.

"You know this man?" asked the short man, who accepted the new intruder without a blink or word. Again I was not sure who was being asked.

"It's Toby," said Sklodovich. "Toby Peters."

Dealer put his gun in the dark silk packet, sat at the edge of his bed, and began to remove the string from his brown paper package as he chewed on his lower lip. Inside the package was a sandwich, which he bagan to eat. There was nothing else in the bag, which supposedly contained clothing.

"What can I do for you?" he said through a mouthful of American cheese.

"Toby wants out, the way you got Ressner out."

Dealer grinned and walked to the window, where he pulled down the shade. Out of the unfurled shade drifted a large sheet of paper. We moved to the bed, where Dealer spread out the paper and Sklodovich assumed an air of rapt attention.

"Our main problem," said Dealer, earnestly pointing to something on the complex chart before us, "is the moat."

"Moat?" I asked.

"The drawbridge is down during the day, but is well guarded," he went on. "At night it is up, but the guard is small because they don't fear an attack from the rear, a move from within the bowels of their own vile creation of terror. I know the mechanism of the bridge, for I've worked on the greasing detail under heavy guard. That mechanism, gentlemen, is the only way. The moat, as you noticed when they brought you in, is not too deep, long, or wide to swim, but it is filled with deadly little fish that can pick a man clean to the bone before he takes three strokes. Therefore one man, you, Ivan, will overpower the drawbridge guard, and you, Toby, will put on the guard's uniform and answer any calls to the guard station while Ivan and I work on the bridge. You can speak their language, can't you?"

"Sure," I said.

"Good. Any questions? Excellent," beamed the man, rolling up the sheet of paper. "Now, as long as they do not put the iron mask back on my head this afternoon, and I doubt if they will, since it caused a strawberry rash last time and they had to work on me for days so I could be viewed without consequence by the Swiss legation and the Red Cross. Gentlemen, until midnight."

The little man removed the robe and climbed into bed after puffing up the pillow. He began to snore before Sklodovich reached the door. We left quietly, closing the door behind us.

"Is that .45 of his loaded?" I asked.

"No mechanism," said Sklodovich, looking down the hall.

"Does he really expect us to come back tonight to escape?"

"I don't know. It doesn't really matter since he wouldn't leave anyway. Besides, I don't want to go. I like it here."

"What do you mean 'he wouldn't leave here anyway?'"

"Dealer can leave whenever he wants to. His door is open. He just won't go out unless a doctor or nurse actually holds his hand and leads him out. He thinks the floor will give way and he'll shoot four floors to the ground. That's his problem."

Leaning against the wall, Sklodovich pulled a key from his pocket.

"A passkey," he said. "Might come in very handy. Dealer slipped it to me."

"I thought you were both idiots," I sighed.

"There's a difference between being insane and being stupid. We aren't stupid."

"I didn't mean . . ."

"No offense taken," said Sklodovich, smiling.

The fluorescent corridor was empty and quiet except for a distant muffle of voices. Sklodovich turned toward the door leading to the roof and I had a sinking, tired feeling down to my knees, which were ready to give way.

"I don't think I can make it over the roof," I whispered, grabbing his arm.

Sklodovich winked and, with a nod of his head, indicated that I should follow him. In a quick-paced follow-the-leader, we bypassed the roof door and made a quick turn to the left down a short corridor with a door at the end. My guide turned the handle with a hairy hand. We walked through the door after he peeped on the other side and found ourselves standing no more than twenty steps from our room, which I had assumed was a gruesome odyssey away.

"Why didn't we just come through there in the first place?" I shouted as I plodded barefoot behind him into the room. "I was almost killed crawling up shafts and onto ledges." He placed the key in the closet on a shelf and covered it with a sheet. I fell exhausted on my bed. I was almost dry by now and wanted to sleep for at least a day, but I was angry enough to glare at the man who had led me on again.

"Many ways of doing things," he said. "Always an easy way, and most people go through life doing things the easy way because it's the only sensible way, but the easy way doesn't always mean anything. To have meaning, things have to be done the hard way, physically, emotionally. If not, you go through life like a vegetable, cooked carrots. Mentally," he said, pointing to his head, "there is no hard way for me anymore, so I do it physically. And hell, I didn't even take you the hardest way. I could have made you slide down a wire in nurse's disguise, but I didn't think you'd make it. Next time, we'll try something a little different. You'll remember that trip for the rest of your life."

"I'll remember every minute here for the rest of my life," I mumbled, placing my arm over my eyes. "Right now I've got a headache and I want some sleep. How much time till midnight?"

"About two hours."

Maybe I fell asleep. Maybe not. It makes little difference because it couldn't have been more than ten minutes later that I removed my arm from my face and saw M.C. next to my bed.

"Checking on you," he said. "Just stay put."

"Five dollars says I can beat you arm-wrestling," said Sklodovich. M.C. watched me ease off the bed and said nothing.

"Five dollars if I lose," Sklodovich went on, going for the money in the closet where he had placed the key. "You don't have to put up a thing."

M.C. glanced casually at the five bills that Sklodovich placed on the night table.

"Five dollars cash," said Sklodovich.

M.C. looked at his watch, walked to the door, and locked it from the inside. A wild, eager flash came into Sklodovich's eyes as he rushed to the closet and searched for something while I watched with curiosity and M.C. paid no attention, but moved the night table out between the two beds.

Sklodovich found what he was looking for and moved to the table, whistling "Beseme Mucho" and grinning. He had two candles in his hand, the kind you use when a fuse blows, and he quickly lighted them and let a little wax drip from each one so they could be placed firmly at two ends of the table.

Whatever he was doing, it didn't surprise M.C., who watched the procedure as if it were a ritual viewed daily.

Sklodovich got into position. Seated on his bed, he placed his right elbow on the table between the two burning candles. M.C. did the same, and their hands clapped together and held. Arm perpendicular between the candles, Sklodovich stopped whistling.

"Say 'go,' Toby," he said, shifting his weight slightly.

Protest would have been useless, and besides, I was fascinated. "Go."

The smooth, black arm and the orangish-white and hairy arm bulged into taut knots, but neither moved. Sklodovich continued to smile happily while M.C. looked neither bored nor interested. If it weren't for the expanding cords of muscle under the tight skin, it would have looked like two men exchanging a strange fraternal grip.

The candles flickered, and one seemed about to go out. I felt that if the flame died, I would roll helplessly onto the floor and under the bed. Whatever they had filled me with was hard to shake.

Time passed, maybe a minute, and a few tiny drops of perspiration appeared on Sklodovich's still happy face, flickering with light from the candles. More time passed, and I thought I heard a sound, a grunt, a sigh from M.C. Still the arms pointed upward. At first I wasn't sure, so I concentrated intently on a point in space a fraction of an inch behind M.C.'s jagged knuckles. A few seconds later I was sure. M.C.'s hand was moving very slowly toward the candle, giving way a fraction of space each second. I saw the flame shine brightly against the black back of his hand only an inch away from the dancing heat. M.C. closed his eyes, the only facial movement he had made. Then, suddenly, the struggle turned and it was Sklodovich who was giving way. When the quivering arms were again pointing toward the ceiling, Sklodovich closed his eyes for another effort. But he still smiled. The table vibrated as the back of Sklodovich's hand slowly approached the flame of the second candle. When the hand was no more than paper thickness from the flame, I could see the dark hairs singeing. Sklodovich said nothing, made no sound as he watched the back of his hand dip into the flame.

M.C. released his hand, snuffed out the two candles with his palm, and stood up.

"We'll have to try that again soon," said Sklodovich, examining his burnt hand. "I'll practice. Don't forget your five dollars."

M.C. turned to Sklodovich and for the first time since I had met him, M.C. smiled.

Sklodovich returned the smile and put the five dollars in the night table.

CHAPTER 13

I don't how much time passed before the door began to open and the hall light cast the shadow of a man on the floor at the foot of our beds. The shadow's body whispered from the door in Sklodovich's familiar voice.

"Toby, get up. It's time."

He pulled open a package and handed crumpled clothing to me. Sklodovich turned the beam toward me so I could put on the white uniform. When I was dressed, he handed me a stethoscope, which I put around my neck, a pair of shoes, which fit fairly well, and a thin, wrinkled raincoat.

"You look just like a doctor," Sklodovich said.

"A pass."

"You know the way you're supposed to go?" Sklodovich asked. I gave an affirmative nod of my head and repeated the instructions he had given me. "The window will be open. I checked it before I came up."

"I'm ready," I said, taking a deep breath and thinking that my freedom was in the hands of an assortment of lunatics.

"Quiet," Sklodovich whispered, putting finger to lips. "Someone's in the hall."

He dived for his bed. The flashlight went out as I crawled quickly under my blanket and closed my eyes. The door opened.

"I know you're still awake." It was M.C.'s voice. "Don't get no ideas. I'm locking this door and I'm going to be right outside of it for the rest of the night."

Sklodovich got up, pat-patted across the floor, and pulled the obviously startled M.C. into the room. Then darkness. Someone had closed the door. I sat listening to the struggle. There was nothing to hear but the panting of two men. It was like earlier arm-wrestling between the candles without the candlelight, and I strained my eyes in the darkness.

"Light," Sklodovich whispered seconds later.

I jumped from my bed, searched Sklodovich's blankets for the flashlight, and turned it on. M.C. and Sklodovich were locked together, teeth clenched, hands clasped overhead, stalemated.

"Go on," Sklodovich said. "I'll hold him. But hurry."

Pride, I assumed, kept M.C. from shouting for help. Given time he would probably overcome the hairy madman, but he wanted to do it himself. How much time would it take? Five minutes, I decided. No longer. Maybe much less.

I wrapped the raincoat tightly around me, got the passkey from the closet, and turned to the door.

"Thanks Ivan," I said, turning out the flashlight."

"My pleasure," he grunted. "Now go."

I stepped into the empty hall and closed the door behind me.

The lights in the hall were dim, and I moved as quickly as I could in the shadow of the walls.

I inched along the wall as I'd seen Lloyd Nolan do in a Mike Shayne movie and looked around the corner where I saw a tired, young nurse at the desk looking at herself in a pocket mirror. It was impossible to get to the room at the end of the hall without being seen by her, and seconds were passing. Then the buzzer rang. In the reflection from the alcove window, I could see her get up and turn her back. With a short gulp, I tiptoed across the open space as fast as I could. The stethoscope almost slipped off my neck. In the safety of the other side of the corridor, I heard the buzzer stop. She had obviously not seen me, but she might now turn to my direction to answer the buzzer call. I ran down the hall to room 421. It had twin, reinforced glass doors, and in the near-total darkness I could make out a long ward room with beds on either side. There was an aisle between the beds, and at the far end I could see another set of double doors. A man was seated at a desk behind those far doors, and behind him was an elevator.

The source of the dim yellow light, which cast a slight and eerie shadow of beds on the wall, came from a desk lamp to the left of the double doors through which I walked. At the desk sat a stocky tree trunk of a man with a flat head, made more flat by his close-cut hair. The white-clad man squinted over his glasses at me as I walked toward him and began to rise, but sat down again.

"Hello, doc," he whispered.

"Hello," I whispered and tried to smile. He looked suspiciously at my mashed face, but the white uniform and stethoscope, which I made sure he could see underneath my open coat, seemed to satisfy him.

"Is there a patient named Barton on this ward?" I asked.

He pushed his glasses back on his large nose and looked at a clipboard before him, running his finger quickly down a list of names on it.

"No, but there is a Bartnik."

"Must have the wrong ward. I could swear they said two."

"This is four, doc. You want two floors below."

"I didn't pay much attention when I got on the elevator. Must have pressed the wrong button. First time I've been here, you know."

"I didn't think I recognized you. You sure it's two you want?"

"You know, now I'm not sure. I'll go down and check it out."

"I'll call records for you, doc, and find out what room this Barton is in."

He reached for the phone on his desk.

"The name is Bartoni, but hold on." I pretended to look at the watch on my wrist. "I'm not going to have time to see him as it is.

I'd better just get down to emergency." He held the phone in his hand for a second, looked at me, and put down the phone.

"Suit yourself, doc." I turned toward the aisle between the two rows of beds. "Doc, do you mind if I check your pass. I mean so I can enter it in the night log."

I walked to the desk, shrugged, and handed the card Sklodovich had given me to the nearsighted orderly.

"Thanks, doc."

"Right," I said as jauntily as I could, took the card back, and hurried down the aisle toward the far double glass doors. His eyes, I could feel, were fixed on my back as I walked away from him, expecting to hear him calling for me to stop. I hurried out of the light from the small desk lamp. About midway across the room I heard a loud voice behind me.

"You mad bastard. Did you think you could get away with this?"

I came close to panic, but I held the metal rail at the foot of the nearest bed. Trapped between two orderlies, I waited for them, or rather the one behind me with the flat head, to leap on my back.

The clap of footsteps echoed behind me in a rush, growing louder and closer, and I turned to see the squat tree trunk coming toward me like a black shadow, a shadow with arms outstretched like an ape to take me in a wild grip and crush me into a small whimper. When he was close enough to touch me, I pulled my doubled fist back, hoping to get in one lucky punch and run like hell. He ducked past me and moved to the side of a patient sitting upright and pointing at me out of the darkness.

"He's not a doctor. He's a mad bastard. I know him."

The man did not shout, but he spoke with anger. He was a little bone bag, that much I could tell but no more, for he was now held in a smothering bear hug by the orderly, whose glasses slipped dangerously down his nose.

"Just calm down now," soothed the orderly, pausing to push his glasses back. "Take it easy. It's all right, doctor. I'll take care of him."

"Right," I said as if this sort of thing happened to me all the time, which might be true if 'all the time' began that afternoon.

"As your Lord God and Savior," hissed the little man in the bed, "I tell you he is not a doctor. I saw him led into this purgatory several aeons ago by that same Delilah who the fallen one sent to tempt and destroy—"

His voice was cut off by the glass door through which I had stepped. Vaguely I thought of how many minutes I might have to go before the alarm was sounded by M.C.

The small space was well lighted to show the elevator and a white-haired, powerful-looking wiry man who sat at a desk before me. A cynical smile greeted me when he looked up from the book he was reading.

"Pass," he said.

I handed him the pass. He examined it and handed it back to me.

"Trouble in there?" he asked. "Heard a little noise."

"The other orderly is taking care of it," I said, pushing the button for the elevator.

"Little fella? 'Bout halfway down on the left?"

"Yes," I said.

"God."

"What?"

"Thinks he's God."

"I see," I said, hoping the elevator would stop grinding and arrive.

"No trouble, doc, but he makes a lot of noise."

"Yes. Typical," I said, not knowing what was typical.

"Yeah," he said as the door for the elevator opened.

"Be seeing you," I said, stepping in.

"Right, doc." The doors closed and I ran my sleeve across my perspiring forehead as I pressed the button marked 2. I leaned against the wall as the elevator went down. I wouldn't have been surprised if the door opened on the third floor and I had found myself facing M.C.

The door opened with a glunking sound, and I stepped into a hallway deserted except for an old Negro woman who leaned against a mop. The floor was covered with wet soap. She watched without expression as I left footprints on her floor in my search for room 321. I forced myself to smile at her and whistle "Dardenella" as I walked down the corridor, looking for the right room and pretending to know exactly where I was going. I found the door I had been told to look for, gave the woman a last smile, and stepped inside.

The staircase was there and I hurried down, feeling the stethoscope thump-thump against my chest. My heart was beating an attack tattoo when I reached the first floor.

With a little confidence restored, I opened the door. A pair of nurses were walking down the hall, and a trio of doctors stood about fifty feet to my right in a huddle. Beyond the doctors I could see the main lobby. As I stepped clearly into the hall, the doctors shifted slightly and one of them, a youngish man as closely as I could judge, seemed to recognize me, change his mind, and then put his hand to his chin as if thinking about something apart from the group topic. He was Dr. Randipur, and the something he was trying to place was me.

I walked through the big room, under the portraits of Drs. Winning of the past, beyond the forest of ferns, around the cluster of doctors, and and through the front door. The drizzle was still coming down. I jumped down the four wooden steps and ran for my Ford.

The door was open. I reached for the glove compartment. The gun was gone. I hoped to hell I could remember how No-Neck Arnie had taught me to wire a car. I remembered. It was damn easy and something every cop and private eye should know. I'd just never had to do it before.

The Ford started noisily, and I whispered to it to be quiet as I backed up and started down the drive with my lights out. I hit a shrub, backed up, and tried again. The stethoscope hit me in the eye, but I kept it on. I still had to get through the gate.

About fifty yards down I turned on my lights, or, I should say, light. The right one didn't work. I eased my way to the gate, hoping that M.C. had not yet raised the alarm and that the same guy who had been on the gate in the morning wasn't on now.

I stopped in front of the closed gate and saw the raincoat-clad figure coming at me from the small lighted booth. He put his face next to the window and I rolled it down, smiling. It wasn't the same guy.

"Bad night for driving, doc," he said. "And you got a headlight out."

"Emergency," I yawned. "You know how it is."

"Yeah," he grinned and moved to open the gate.

I gave him a wave and counted slowly to keep myself from tearing down the road, but the count kept going faster, and I couldn't hold it back. By ten I was moving as fast as the Ford would take me away from the Winning Institute.

CHAPTER 14

Rosie turned down the raincoat and stethoscope as collateral for the money I owed her. She didn't even ask why I was dressed like a doctor, only shook her head and let some air out between her teeth to indicate I was the damndest practical joker she had ever met. She filled my gas tank, gave me another five-dollar loan, and I promised to get it back to her within the next week even if I had to sell the car to do it, which would have made little sense, since I already owed more than a century note on the damn thing. I rummaged through a box of clothes left by Rosie's long-gone husband and came up with a not-too-bad-fitting pair of brown pants, a flannel shirt, and a blue sweater with one hole just under the left armpit. That was all free. I gulped down some coffee and a roll Rosie pushed in my hands just as the sun started to come up. I was coming out of a nightmare, and I wondered how much of it had really happened.

Mae West's ranch in the valley was the closest place on my list, so I headed for it well within the speed limit and expecting to be pulled over by a state cop as an escaped loony with no driver's license. I had a lot of thinking to do, which was not good for my health or well-being. My best ideas seemed to come not when I added things together but when they stewed somewhere deep and bubbled up by themselves. Not much made sense at the moment. My head wasn't throbbing anymore, though my scalp seemed to be shrinking. My back seemed fine so far.

When I pulled up in front of West's ranch a few hours later, I was hungry and worried. Ressner had done a good job of getting me out of the way. Part of it was show, but part of it was because he had some plan that, to quote what some people attributed to Sam Goldwyn, included me out.

Seeing Jeremy's bulk filling the doorway and an unseen weight pushing down his brow made me think that whatever Ressner had planned had already happened. I jumped out of the car and jogged to Jeremy.

"Too late," he said softly.

"He killed Mae West?" I croaked.

Jeremy looked up at me sadly, "Killed . . . no. You're too late to help. He . . . it . . . came last night. Dressed like that. I was drinking apricot juice in the kitchen. The two—"

"Dizzy and Daffy," I said. "The beefcake bookends."

"Yes," continued Jeremy. "They were on an errand. Miss West opened the door before I could get there. He had a knife. I got to the doorway in the living room as fast as I could, but I was too late."

"Jeremy, this is all very dramatic, but what were you too late for? How badly was she hurt?"

"She wasn't. She cracked him in the head with a book of Keats's poetry I had given her to read. Ressner, or whoever it was, fell back, holding his face and nose bleeding. He looked ready for another try, saw me, and ran for the car. I couldn't catch him even though he was wearing high heels."

"A dark Packard?" I said.

"Yes, I think so," said Jeremy, rubbing the top of his smooth bald head. "You should have seen her standing in that doorway, her hands on her hips. She is quite a woman, quite a person. I'm working on a poem about her, Toby."

"Keep at it, Jeremy. Where is she now?"

He guided me upstairs and knocked at the door. Mae West's voice came through.

"Who might that be?"

"Toby Peters," I said.

"*Entrez*," she said, and I did with Jeremy behind me.

She was seated at a white dressing table looking at herself in a mirror. On her head was a massive fluffy peach-colored feather hat.

"Therapy," she explained, putting the hat to the side. "I meditate for an hour in the morning and then try on hats. You should try it sometime."

"I'd be beautiful in that hat," I said,

She laughed, a hoarse guffaw.

"I meant the meditation," she said. "Taught to me by a genuine yoga who could be a real charmer when he wanted to be."

"Ressner came back last night," I prompted.

She turned to look at me and motioned to an old French movie settee. It was frail and hard, and I hoped Jeremy wouldn't join me on it. The room was full of mirrors, and Mae West watched me looking around with an amused smile on her face.

"Fun and games," she said.

I looked at her.

"This Ressner fella," she explained. "He parted your scalp?"

"Right."

"He's not prone to *empressement*," she mused, raising her eyebrows. She looked anything but scared, and I wondered why.

"He doesn't scare you?"

"A little," she admitted, "but I'm at a bad point in my life and career. The divorce business is getting me, the protests about my work. I'm not sure whether I'm coming or going and who I'm taking with me. Let me give you some advice. Don't ever work with W. C. Fields. Most de-pressing experience I've ever had. In fact, my advice is to stay away from comics. They're a self-pitying brood."

"Aren't you a comic?" I asked.

"I am a national institution, a risqué treasure being stifled by the repression old Sigmund told us about but we were too inhibited to listen to," she said with a smile. "I'm so darned clean in *Chickadee* my own mother wouldn't have recognized me. So, all this excitement came just when I needed a little stimulation. Gave old Jeremy here a rise too."

Jeremy, standing by the door, looked at and away from me.

"I don't think Ressner will be coming back," I said. "Not for now. I think he'll go for another target."

"Who," said West, "said it was Ressner last night?"

"It wasn't the same . . ?"

"I don't know," she ventured, getting up from the table and admiring her flowered amber dress in one of the large mirrors. She patted her stomach and breathed deeply to pull it in, and it stayed there. "Never really got a look at the gentleman the other night and I didn't really get a good look last night. Just saw this poor imitation with a knife and I didn't wait for dialogue. I could have used a real Grecian urn."

"If it's all right with you," I said, getting up, "Jeremy will go back to town with me. I think I've got a line on Ressner and I may need his help. We'll wait here until your houseboys get back, and I'll call the local cops and tell them there's been a threat on your life. They'll give you about a day of coverage."

"Speaking of the john-darmes," she said, turning to me. "How is the Panda taking this."

"The Panda?"

"Phil," she explained with a grin.

"Panda?" I guess he does look a little like a constipated Panda at that. "He's doing just fine," I lied.

"Give him my best when this all blows over," she said. "And don't forget to send me a bill for your services."

"No bill," I said. "I told you, this is a favor. I'll take something in payment, though."

She looked up at me and let the grin open into a comic leer as she looked over at the bed without moving her head.

"And what might that be?"

"That hat. The flowery peach thing you were trying on a few minutes ago," I said.

"You sure your scalp is pasted back on?" she said, looking from me to Jeremy and then back again.

"I'm sure. I need a wedding present for an old friend."

She shrugged, turned around, put the hat in a round, white box, tied it neatly, and handed the whole thing to me.

"My pleasure," she said, touching my hand. I took the bulky box and turned to go.

I hurried down the stairs, looking for a phone, with Jeremy right behind.

"Magnificent," he said.

"It'll do," I answered.

"I didn't mean the hat."

We moved into the kitchen. I found a phone and called the local police. Then we waited impatiently for the local cops and Dizzy and Daffy to return.

Meanwhile Mae West rested blissfully above.

Jeremy read me part of his poem in progress about her, told me how many islands we had lost in the Pacific overnight, and made us a stack of egg salad sandwiches on white with a pair of beers and some chunks of white cheese.

Maybe someday when I had the time I'd put together a gourmet cookbook of the favorite foods of detective Toby Peters. Nero Wolfe would quake with envy.

When the cops showed up, hands on their guns, a pair of burly over-the-hillers, I stood back while Jeremy introduced himself as a friend of the family, said that Mae West was sleeping off the trauma upstairs, and that Dizzy and Daffy would explain the whole thing, since they were just walking in with full armloads of groceries.

Both of them looked dumbfounded.

"This is your big moment, boys," I said. "Miss West wants police protection for the rest of the day. Tell the tale."

Jeremy and I went through the door, leaving the duo holding the bags, while the cops waited for an explanation. They'd probably have to wake Mae up to charm the cops and repair the damage, but I had other damage to prevent.

I drove toward Los Angeles and told Jeremy the whole story. He was especially charmed by Sklodovich and considered a way of communicating with him to give him a better exercise regime.

"Dynamic tension is good for body tone," he said, "but you've got to sweat and work those muscles and cleanse the body. The world is not clean, Toby. It is not clean. What we must do is keep our mind and bodies clean. Not in the conventional Puritanical sense, but in the sense of removing the pollution of thought and atmosphere."

"You said a mouthful, toots," I agreed. "But what about Ressner?"

"I wonder why he has suddenly taken to violence?" said Jeremy.

"Dr. Winning's words or close to them. He was cooped up in that booby hatch for four years. I was there less than a day, and those doctors and patients almost turned me into a cross-eyed kangaroo."

"Perhaps," said Jeremy. "But something is missing. The woman who said she was your sister who called the institute?"

"Ressner is pretty good on voices," I reminded him. "Remember that night at the pool?"

"Something is still missing," he insisted.

"Jeremy, I'm having enough trouble keeping this simple. Let's just get over to Paramount and do our damned best to save Cecil B. De Mille's life."

We made what I hoped would be a brief stop at my boardinghouse. Jeremy waited in the car while I snuck up the steps to avoid a confrontation with Mrs. Plaut. I wasn't dressed for a Paramount party.

There was a note pinned to my door. In scrawled red crayon, unmistakably Mrs. Plaut, it said, PLEASE REMOVE THAT JUNK METAL FROM YOUR ROOM OR YOURSELF.

I went in and examined the bumper lying neatly on the floor. I hadn't had time to fight with No-Neck Arnie about it, the car radio, the gas gauge, and my future transportation. I deposited the hatbox on my bed and went to my closet. There wasn't much wardrobe left to pick from.

I selected a pair of brown pants and a white shirt with a bad stain on the back, which wouldn't show if I didn't have to take off the too-small waiter's jacket that I pulled from the back of the closet. It had a stale smell and wasn't mine. It had been left in the closet by the waiter who used to live in the room. He had been tall enough, but his arms were shorter than mine. To distract the world, I put on the Christmas tie Shelly had given me two years earlier, which I had never worn. It was light blue with the letters *ADA* sewn in pink. I suspected that it had been a giveaway at an American Dental Association convention. Shelly had told me that it meant "Always Dependable Ally."

I looked at myself in the bathroom mirror and knew that if the Japanese were searching for an easy target, they'd have it as soon as I stepped into the street.

Gunther popped his head out of the door as I started to leave.

"Toby," he began, and then his little mouth dropped open as he looked at my costume.

"Right, Gunther," I said seriously. "I've got to get to Paramount. De Milles's in trouble."

Gunther, who spent his money on neatly tailored handmade conservative suits, couldn't take his eyes from my tie as he spoke.

"Mrs. Plaut is most irate," he said. "Most irate. I told her that the large piece of metal was a patriotic modern sculpture done by a serviceman."

"Very inventive, Gunther," I said and meant it.

"She, however, did not accept my explanation. I do not have your gift of dissembled conversation," he said a bit apologetically.

"Stick with me," I consoled, "and you'll pick it up. Want to join us?"

"Yes, perhaps," he said with animation. "Hans Mulsin has waited two hundred years to be translated into English. He can wait another few hours. I'll get my coat."

I looked at the stairway nervously, expecting Mrs. Plaut, and waited. Gunther emerged, wearing a neat Chesterfield coat, Homburg, and a cane.

"We are going to a fine party, are we not?" he said.

"It is now," I said and led the way down the stairs and out of the house.

Jeremy and Gunther exchanged greetings, and with great dignity, Gunther put his hand on his Homburg and climbed into the small space behind us.

We were at Paramount ten minutes later, where a guard at the gate stopped us and looked into the car. He was an old-timer named Belzer, whom I met once or twice back in the days I was working Warner. Most of the people working the studios were old-timers now. The young-timers were in different uniforms.

"Toby Peters, is it?" he said. His cap was well down on his forehead when he looked into the car and exchanged nods with Jeremy and Gunther, who peeked over the backseat along with the top of his silver cane.

Little tufts of white hair had sprouted from Belzer's ears since I last saw him. It was decorative.

"Couldn't believe it was you when Mr. De Mille left the list here for the get-together. Spotted you right away," Belzer went on. "How have you been?"

"Failing to make a living," I said. He looked at my suit and tie and the Ford and shook his head. He believed me.

"Your friends on the guest list?" he said.

A car pulled up alongside it, and Chester Morris stuck his head out of the window. Belzer waved him on.

"They're my partners," I said. "We're here to protect De Mille from a maniac named Ressner."

I described Ressner to him, and he tried to think, but a lot of people had come through that gate and Ressner could have been many of them, male or female.

"Don't remember, but that's no guarantee one way or another," he said. "Drive on in. Go to the end of this street and then sharp to the left. Should be a whole bunch of cars parked. Find yourself a space and follow the crowd."

In the rearview mirror I could see that the car behind us was driven by Madeleine Carroll. It was going to be some party.

CHAPTER 15

We parked, got out, and passed Chester Morris, following the crowd into the clear May afternoon. The woman with Morris looked at us over her shoulder and nodded. Morris glanced at us and said, "Must be entertainment." He grinned at us and we grinned back. We did turn out to be the entertainment, but not quite the comedy act he had in mind.

In a studio full of famous faces, we held our own in drawing attention. So I decided that we should separate. I described Ressner to Jeremy and Gunther again, though I knew my description wouldn't be much good. The real trick was to find and stick close to De Mille and look for anyone who might have a hidden knife, though we weren't even sure if Ressner would stick to his familiar weapon.

The crowd flowed, and I moved to the side. In a few seconds, I lost sight of Gunther and Jeremy. My guess, and I was pretty good at crowds from my studio premiere days, was that there were about four or five hundred people in the space into which we were being corralled.

That space looked familiar to me, and I tried to imagine it without the modern dressed people. It was the outdoor set of King Richard's courtyard for *The Crusades*.

On the stone wall to the side hung a huge poster with a cartoon sailor holding some pieces of paper. The red, white, and blue lettering read, BUY BONDS NOW. DO YOUR PART. WE'RE DOING OURS.

I leaned against a wooden post next to a plaster of Paris fountain and scanned the crowd.

"Looking for someone particular to give the evil eye or will anyone do?" came a voice behind me.

I knew the voice and didn't want to turn, but there wasn't any choice now. A hefty guy said "Excuse me" as he moved past looking for a spot to perch, and I looked back at Brenda Stallings. Her nose was about a foot from mine, and she looked tired. She was wearing a tan suit and silver earrings, but she wasn't shining. She held a purse, and I wondered if there might be a tiny gun in it. I had succeeded in being around and involved when two men in her life lost theirs.

"I was trying to save Talbott," I explained.

She shook her head, gritting her even white teeth, and examined me from bandage to ADA tie to tight waiter's jacket to baggy pants.

"What are you dressed up for?" she gasped.

"Comic relief?" I tried.

Her right hand went up to her eyes, and she began to shake. I reached for her and touched her shoulder.

"I don't know if I'm laughing or crying," she said, taking down her hand and reaching in her purse for a handkerchief. "Probably both."

"Makes sense," I said, continuing to scan the crowd for signs of Ressner. "It's like that for me almost all the time."

She looked at me with those intense blue eyes filled with tears and said, "What do you wind up doing?"

"Smiling," I said. "Can I get you a drink? I think I see some guys circulating."

"Sure," she sighed. "Why not."

I inched through the crowd past a character actress with no chin, whom I recognized but to whom I couldn't put a name. A lot of the people I made my way past looked like producers or bankers, money people.

C. Aubrey Smith and I reached for same drink on the tray.

"After you, dear chap," he said genially, trying to read the letters on my tie. He took a glass of wine, touched his big white moustache, and said, "Mind if I ask?" pointing at my tie.

"American Defense Always," I explained.

"Quite right," he agreed and turned away.

I made my way through the crowd back to Brenda Stallings and handed her the wineglass. I took a sip of my own and watched her down hers in one tilt of the head. Rather than go back through the crowd, I gave her mine. She took it and finished it off before my hand was back at my side.

I took the empty glasses and placed them both in the pool at the base of the plaster of Paris fountain.

"Toby," Brenda said over the murmur of the crowd. "Do me a

favor. Never, never see or talk to me again." She touched my cheek.

"I'll try," I said, and she disappeared as something began to stir behind me. I turned. On a low platform of wood raised above the crowd stood a man at a microphone. A sharp buzz came over a loudspeaker, and the man dressed in a tuxedo spoke with a sputtering S because he was standing too close to the mouthpiece. Radio was not his medium.

"Ladies and gentlemen, please. Your attention. We want to welcome you here today on behalf of Paramount Pictures. It is my pleasure to introduce our host for the afternoon, Mr. Cecil B. De Mille." De Mille climbed to the platform and moved forward with a tall dark-suited old man, who looked something like a cross between an undertaker and a clean-shaven Abe Lincoln. De Mille was wearing tan kickers, a white shirt, and light brown jacket.

"Ladies and gentleman," he said after the applause had died. He spoke slowly, clearly, a man well at home with a microphone. "It is my distinct honor to share this platform today with the man who may be most responsible for the industry in which we work, the man who turned a technology into an art, the true pioneer of the film medium, Mr. David Wark Griffith."

Griffith stepped forward with a small smile to the applause and leaned into the microphone.

"I thank you, C.B.," he said. "And I thank you especially for the opportunity to urge all of these loyal Americans to support our war effort."

De Mille stepped up and made it quite clear that the little presentation had been rehearsed.

"Yes, D.W. We're at a crucial point in the war being fought all around us, a point where every dollar and every bit of effort and sacrifice is needed to see us through to victory. I'd like to see us sell a million dollars in bonds right here. This afternoon. I know you have the power to do it, just as I know America has the will to win."

"C.B.," said Griffith in distinct cultured tones. "I'd like to start the camera rolling with the purchase of a one-hundred-dollar bond.

De Mille applauded and I wondered if Griffith could afford a hundred-buck token payment. I'd heard from a friend that the old man had been reduced to noncredited consulting at Hal Roach's studio.

"Now," went on C.B. "Mr. Griffith and I and our volunteers will circulate among you. There are plenty of refreshments, and many of you have kindly agreed to perform for us through the afternoon. So enjoy yourselves, open your hearts and purses, your souls and wallets, and help us to make this an afternoon for which Hollywood can be proud."

More applause as De Mille and Griffith waved and left the podium to Kay Kyser who adjusted his glasses and said, "Hi you all."

Before he could call Ish Kabible to the stand or start his band playing, I pushed through the crowd to find De Mille.

People were flocking around one of several tables set up to sell bonds. I moved behind one of the tables as the music began. I thought I recognized the voice of Ginny Simms singing "Who's Sorry Now," but I didn't spot De Mille.

Someone touched my arm, and I looked down at Gunther. I had to bend down to hear him over the music and voices.

"Toby, did you not tell me that Miss West struck this Ressner in the face last night?"

"Right," I said.

"There is a waiter serving behind that punch bowl with a bandage on his nose. It may mean nothing, but . . ."

I hurried in the direction of the punch bowl as indicated by Gunther. The going was slow.

I passed Bing Crosby, who was holding something small up to a young man and saying, "Will you look at that?"

The table with the punch bowl was long and covered with a white tablecloth and little punch glasses. Behind it stood not one but three waiters serving. One of them, indeed, had a bandage on his nose. His hair was dark and long, and he sported a black moustache, but it was Ressner without a doubt, the same man who had appeared in my office and told me he was Dr. Winning. I tried to ease around a chubby guy, who had one foot propped up to tie his shoe.

Ressner looked up at the right or wrong moment and spotted me. His eyes made it clear that I wasn't supposed to be there. I was supposed to be locked up in a booby hatch outside of Fresno.

He turned and ducked into the crowd behind him. I followed.

For four or five minutes I plowed through celebrities asking me questions about my tie and people who didn't want to move or be moved. No Ressner. I gave up and looked for De Mille. Instead I spotted Jeremy talking to a matronly woman.

"Romanticism is returning now in full flower with the young English poets," he was saying as I grabbed his arm. He excused himself, and I told him to help me find and keep an eye on De Mille. I told him about Ressner and his disguise, and we separated again.

About four minutes later I spotted De Mille again, this time without Griffith, as he returned to the platform and took the microphone.

"We're doing very well," he said. "But we can do better. Open those hearts as I know you can."

"Blasphemer," came a shout from behind De Mille. The roar of the crowd stopped as everyone looked up. A figure climbed on the stage. He was dressed like a hermit and carrying a wooden staff. He also had a bandage over his nose.

De Mille's "Oh my God," was barely audible over the speaker because he had turned his head.

The crowd waited anxiously, wondering what this piece of entertainment would be. I tried to muscle through the crowd as Ressner stepped toward De Mille with his staff raised.

I could see Jeremy to my right, muscling his way forward with more success than I was having, but still too far to get there before Ressner had a chance to strike out with his staff. The people around the platform must have thought it was part of an act, too, because no one moved to give De Mille help.

I kept driving forward and glanced up to see De Mille standing quite resolutely with his feet apart, waiting for Ressner.

I was at the foot of the platform when Ressner raised the staff and shouted, "For all the filth that you have put on the screen and the defilement of the Lord, I shall smite thee."

"Your knowledge of the Bible," I could hear De Mille say, "is as weak as your performance. Now . . ."

Ressner was about to bring the staff down on De Mille's head, and neither Jeremy nor I was near enough to act. But instead of the heavy stick swooping through the air, it went flying high into the crowd, and Ressner tripped forward.

At the edge of the platform I could now see Gunther, his cane extended. I guessed that he had climbed up and hit Ressner in the shin. It was a good guess. Ressner turned in fury toward Gunther, who tried to scramble away. He almost made it. Ressner caught him by the collar and pulled him up where everyone could see. De Mille moved to help, but Ressner lifted Gunther and flung him into the crowd. People went down like lined-up blocks when Gunther's body struck, and Ressner leaped off the back of the platform into the crowd.

The applause and cheers were deafening and one man shouted, "Magnificent show, C.B."

A woman's voice confirmed, "You might expect something like this from C.B. Wonderful dramatic sense. Wonderful."

De Mille quickly climbed from the podium, and I caught a glimpse of Jeremy burrowing around the crowd in pursuit of Ressner. I went for Gunther, who was being held up and dusted off by a pretty young girl.

"You were wonderful," she said.

"How are you, Gunther?" I asked.

"While I prefer not to be publicly conspicuous, as you well know, Toby," he said, looking for his Homburg, "I am well trained in tumbling and well able to absorb the fall and the indignity. The mother of this child upon whom I landed is in some anguish."

The pretty girl remembered her mother, pulled her fascinated eyes from Gunther, and went to the woman, who had been seated in a chair and now looked as if Jim Thorpe had belted her in the solar plexus.

I took up the chase of Ressner, passing D. W. Griffith on the way, who was saying, "Carol Dempster. Without a doubt. Carol Dempster."

The crowd thinned at the edge of the set, and I moved between two buildings in the general direction I had seen Jeremy and Ressner take off. Nothing. I went to my right and found myself circling back toward the party and the set from *The Crusades*.

I climbed some wooden stairs and found myself on the tower over the party. In front of me, about fifty feet down on the wooden planking, Jeremy was advancing on Ressner, who had nowhere to go.

I ran forward. Ressner moved to the edge of the railing some thirty feet above the crowd. No one seemed to spot him from below. Jeremy took a step to the side, and I could see the too-calm look on his face. I didn't like it.

Ressner struck out with his fist and hit Jeremy cleanly on the chin, but Jeremy paid no attention. Ressner backed up his last step and threw a punch toward Jeremy's neck. Jeremy ignored it.

"I should have been a star," shouted Ressner in Jeremy's face. "I am a great actor. This is an unfair world."

Jeremy's answer was to grab the front of Ressner's hairy costume and lift him up. I stopped about ten feet away when Jeremy lifted Ressner over his head as Ressner had done to Gunther. There was no doubt about what Jeremy had in mind. He was going to fling the madman into the crowd below.

Ressner looked over at me with a combination of fear and anticipation. It might mean his death, but it also would mean his greatest moment. All of Hollywood was gathered for his big scene.

"Jeremy," I said above the band that had started playing "Darktown Strutter's Ball." "Gunther is all right. Not even a bruise."

Jeremy's response was to hoist Ressner even higher.

"That's what he wants you to do, Jeremy," I said. "That will be his big splash in the movie world. It's the death wish he's been after."

Jeremy hesitated, and I took another step forward.

"It'll hurt him a lot more to go back to the Winning Institute or to go on trial," I said.

With that, Jeremy turned and threw Ressner on the wooden planking at my feet. The madman landed on his back, bounced, groaned, and rolled on his side.

"And what of my satisfaction?" said Jeremy, rubbing his hands.

"Get it through poetry," I said, grabbing Ressner's arm.

Jeremy nodded at the wisdom of my remark and helped me drag Ressner's unmartyred form back down the walkway and into the nearest office where I could make a phone call to my brother.

Ressner's thin brown hair fell over his pale blue eyes. Jeremy had seated him at a desk chair on little rollers. Scratching his stomach once or twice through his itchy hair shirt, Ressner began to rock back and forth with a satisfied grin.

"Why'd you kill them?" I asked, looking at the walls of the small room. There was nothing on three of them. On the fourth was a large photograph of an old man with a high starched collar, who looked at all three of us without humor.

"I haven't killed them yet," Ressner said in a slight singsong voice that, I think, was intended to sound like Clark Gable.

"Grayson and Talbott," I tried.

"I've never met Grayson, and Talbott, when we went out for a drink, seemed a most amiable fellow," the Clark Gable voice went on.

"And De Mille?" I asked.

"I did not intend to kill him," he said, switching to Frank Morgan. "I was going to miss him with the staff after my scene was ended. That would show him acting. I'd have him, the whole audience, Hollywood in my hand." He held up his right hand, stopped rocking for a few seconds, looked at his hand, and then rocked again.

"The money, where did you get the money?" I went on.

"What money?" The voice had changed, and Ressner had one eyebrow lifted.

"The money you gave me to find you when you pretended you were Winning. The money to get new clothes. The money to buy gas, hire someone to call Dr. Winning, and send a check to Winning to put me under observation at the institute. That money."

Ressner's eyebrow went up, and he pursed his lips. I almost recognized the impression but not quite.

"I'm not at liberty at the moment to say," he said.

"Who are you doing?"

"Franchot Tone," he said, shaking his head at my ignorance. "I'll answer no more questions. I don't betray those who serve me with loyalty. Am I going back to the institute?"

"I guess so," I said. "Sklodovich and Dealer send their regards."

Ressner kept rocking and shrugged. Jeremy had turned his back and was looking out the window. An idea was beginning to form somewhere in my well-kneaded brain.

Phil and Steve Seidman arrived about thirty minutes later, about at the point where I could take no more of Ressner's rambling. His answers to my questions consisted of a look of superior knowledge and a discussion of the quality of his performance of the past few days. I wasn't in the mood to be an appreciative critic, considering that I had been the principal supporting actor. I got nothing reasonable out of him about the murders, and I gave up. I decided to leave him for Phil's gentle touch and charm.

"This is him?" asked Phil, looking down at Ressner.

"It's him," I acknowledged.

"Two murders," Phil said through a tired smile. "We're going to give you a nice home where you won't bother people anymore."

"I have killed no one," said Ressner, adjusting his hair shirt with dignity and turning away.

Phil's fist shot out and hit him behind the ear. Ressner flew into the corner. Phil was about to take a few steps over and give Ressner a real cause for martyrdom when Seidman stepped in front of him.

"Phil," Seidman said quietly.

Jeremy stood in the corner with his arms folded, watching silently.

"I don't like him," Phil said. "He could have killed Mae West, did kill two people, and you know what they're going to do? They're going to send him to some funny farm for a lifetime vacation. Well, maybe he can bring a few memories with him to make his nights uncomfortable."

"Take it easy, Panda," I said, moving to his side.

He turned on me with close to the hatred he had shown for Ressner.

"What did you call me?" he said, though he had heard it clearly.

"Brother," I said. "I called you brother."

"And why the hell are you dressed up like that?" he said pointing at my clothes.

"I'm part of the entertainment," I explained.

"You're a damned embarrassment," Phil said, shaking off Seidman and giving one final glare at Ressner. "Put him in the car and get him down to the station. We'll ask him a few more questions before we turn him over to the lockup."

Phil didn't say anything else to me. I almost called him back and told him that there was something else, that the case wasn't quite over. But it could wait. There were a few things I wanted to do first.

I drove Jeremy back to the Farraday and thanked him. Gunther invited him to have dinner with us, but Jeremy declined. He was a day behind on keeping the Farraday a step away from extinction.

I dropped Gunther off at Mrs. Plaut's and picked up my bumper and the hatbox. I took the hatbox to the TWA office where Anne worked with Ralph. I didn't know if she would keep working now, and I was sure she'd still be on her honeymoon. I jotted down a little note and asked the woman at the reception desk to see that Anne got the late wedding present. I didn't know what she'd make of the hat. I hoped she'd look at it and laugh and then keep it somewhere. On the other hand, she might just produce that look of weary exasperation at the child-man she had once lived with and throw the whole thing in the garbage. I drove to Arnie's.

No-Neck was a tougher customer. I insisted that he put the bumper back on, fix the radio and the gas gauge for no additional charge. He insisted on some of the money I owed him. I didn't even have my gun to threaten him with or hock for partial payment.

We struck a deal. He'd fix the car the next day. I'd find a way to pay what I owed by the end of the next week, and I'd collect on his stack of late payments and bad debts. Knowing some of Arnie's clients, it wasn't much of a deal, but it was the only one I had. I left him holding the bumper while I climbed into the car. I still had a long trip to make.

CHAPTER 16

With less than two bucks in nickels and dimes I had scraped from my sofa pillows and pockets, I drove back out of town. I knew a guy named Trencherman in the secretary of state's office who could probably get me a duplicate driver's license reasonably fast if I begged him, but I had no time for phone calls. The begging didn't bother me.

It was late in the afternoon when I pulled into Dot's Dixie Gas Station and hit the horn. It was the first time I had tried the horn. It didn't work. I got out and shouted, adding the damned horn to my list of negotiable items to bring up to Arnie. Arnie had almost as much to answer for as General Franco.

"Anybody here?" I called.

Tommy the mongrel came loping out from behind the station, stopped, sat down, and looked at me. A few paces behind him came Dot himself, hands plunged in his overalls, pipe in the corner of his mouth, lost in thought.

"What can I do you . . . it's you, the fella who left with the midget," he said.

"It's me," I acknowledged. "How about some gas? I'll make a deal. This tie for three gallons."

Dot walked up to look at the tie. The dog moved to his side and joined him.

"What's the ADA for?" he asked.

"Association of Defenders of America," I answered proudly.

"Two gallons," he said. "On account of I was in the service with Sergeant Alvin York, the number one defender of America ever lived."

"I remember you mentioning it," I said as he moved to the pump. "What you do with my old wreck?"

Dot chuckled slyly and nodded toward the rear of the station.

"Fixing her up back there. Welding the transmission back, a few hoses and such, and she'll be—"

"Good as new," I finished.

"Nope, never that, but worth a couple of hundred and probably in better shape than what you're driving here."

I bought a Whiz bar and bottle of Pepsi, for which I paid precious cash, bid Dot and Tommy farewell, and went on about my business.

Plaza Del Lago glittered green in the dusk when I came over that last hill and into the dry valley. I didn't stop or even slow down at Cal's General Store. I didn't need information and couldn't pay for services. Besides, I knew where I was going even if I wasn't sure what I could find there.

The porches of the two hotels were empty. People were inside eating their dinner and drinking Poodle Springs water. I went on to the Grayson house and parked just about where I had the last time.

Next to the house sat the Packard. The sun was almost gone for the day, and somewhere out in the desert an animal went crazy yelping. I looked once at the Joshua, walked up to the door, and knocked.

The door opened, and I gave my best Sunday-go-to-hell grin at the moustached man in front of me, who put his hand to his bushy hair, looked as if he had been caught with his hand where it shouldn't have been, and said, "Mr. Peters."

"I thought my name was Pevsner," I said to Dr. Winning, giving him time to grab an idea or two.

"I'm truly sorry about that," he said, sounding more than truly sorry. "As soon as you left, I did some checking. Your story was absolutely true. I'll have someone drop your clothes and your gun at your office."

"Can I come in, or do you just want to close the door and pretend I never came?"

He hesitated for an instant and then stepped back to let me pass.

"The Graysons have been under a great deal of stress with this," he said. "I've been trying to help with Mrs. Grayson."

"Who is it?" came Delores Grayson's voice as she stepped into the hall. She was wearing a pair of white slacks and a white sweater and looked as if she had just stepped out of an ad for Woodbury soap. "You?"

"I seem to be welcome wherever I go," I said, stepping forward before someone shoved me out of the door.

"The state police are looking for you," she said nervously.

"You mean you didn't tell them I didn't kill Grayson?" I asked.

"I will," she said. "But I've been so . . ."

I shook my head no and closed one eye to show how lame her tale was and moved past her into the living room.

"Take your time and think up a story," I said. "I've got all night. Why not practice by telling me how the Packard got back."

Winning answered without missing a beat.

"Jeffrey Ressner called Delores and told her where it was. I stopped for it in Los Angeles and drove it back, Actually, it's rather fortunate that you came by. Maybe you can give me a lift back to town."

"Maybe," I said, sitting in a hardback chair. "Where's the grieving widow?"

Delores stepped forward and bit her lower lip.

"Mother is resting in the other room. This has all been—"

"A bag of Poodle piss," I finished for her. "Oh mom," I shouted, "could you paddle out here for a second or two?"

"Is someone there?" came the Billie Burke voice I recognized from the phone.

"It's me, Thor," I said. "I common to fix things all up you bet."

She was shorter than her daughter, maybe fifty, with gray-brown hair and wearing a sensible black widow's suit. She was a good-looking woman with the kind of blow-away charm that powerful men sometimes like to protect.

"I don't really understand," she said, turning to Doc Winning and Delores for an explanation.

"To tell the truth, Mrs. Grayson, I don't really understand it all myself," I said. "Delores, you think you can brew some of that delicious coffee of yours?"

"There's coffee on the stove right now," she said, glaring at me. "I think you should leave, or we'll be forced to call the police. You're disturbing my mother."

"I don't think I'm doing much for your peace of mind either," I went on.

"You're enjoying this scene, aren't you, Mr. Peters?" Winning said, moving to sit across from me while Mrs. Grayson fluttered to a place next to him.

"Yes," I admitted. "Once a year or so I get a moment like this and I like to roll it around on my tongue like the good brandy I can't afford."

"Are you hinting at something?" Delores said.

"A cup of fine coffee. Take your time. You won't miss anything. I've got a ghost story to start, and then we can all take turns finishing it."

She looked at Winning, who nodded at her, and she hurried off to the back of the house.

"Mister Thor," Jeanette Grayson began.

"His name is Peters, Jeanette," Winning corrected.

She recognized my name and shut up. We sat looking at each other for two or three minutes till Delores came in and handed me a cup of coffee.

"I put in two spoons of sugar and some cream," she said.

"You have a good memory," I said, sipping the coffee.

"Mr. Peters, you are annoying." She folded her arms and sat.

"It took me some time to figure the whole thing out," I began between sips. "I probably still have some of it wrong, but I think it makes sense."

"Go on," said Winning.

"First, I should tell you that Ressner has been caught."

That got them. They looked at one another, and Winning held up a calming hand.

"That's good," he said. "I hope he hasn't been hurt."

"He's fine. Just about now he's probably telling his tale to two Los Angeles Homicide cops with a lot of muscle and very little sympathy."

"My father should have a lawyer," Delores Ressner shouted, getting up and going to the phone.

"That's a good idea," I said. "I've got a good one named Marty Leib. He's a bit expensive, but we won't spare the dollars where Dad is concerned, will we?"

"Mr. Peters," piped up Mrs. Grayson. "This sarcasm is uncalled for."

"Let me tell it and any of you chime in to correct me," I began. Delores put the phone down and listened.

"Somewhere during the last four years while Jeffrey Ressner was going his mad merry way in the Winning Institute, one of you, probably Doc Winning, got the idea of using Ressner to make a few million dollars," I began. "Ressner would be allowed to escape. He'd go looking for his benevolent wife and loving daughter.

"It worked fine to that point. He got in touch with Delores and told her he was at the Los Olvidados Hotel. She went to see him and let him hatch his scheme against Mae West. It was all right if he got caught. It would show the world how mad he was, and you could let him escape again. As it turned out, he wasn't caught. He ran into me and got away.

"That was a problem. I tracked him down through the Engineer's Thumbs and you knew I might catch up with him before the whole scheme went through. So you got him to go into his Dr. Winning act with me, throw me off, use me. He thought he was toying with me. What he was doing was setting me up as a witness, a witness to a pair of murders I'd pin on him. How am I doing so far?"

"This is ridiculous," Mrs. Grayson said, standing up and almost weeping.

"Right," I agreed, "but close to what happened. I came running up here, and Delores intercepted me, telling me that Daddy was in the next room talking to the mean old stepfather. I swallowed it whole and went in. Here's the point where I have some choices.

Any one of the three of you could have put the knife in Grayson. I'm putting my money on Delores, who did him in and then came out in her bathing suit to greet me and serve me a cup of coffee. My guess is you killed him when you saw me coming up the driveway and hustled Ressner into the Packard to make a run for it and look guilty as hell. Is this coffee poisoned?"

"I'm sorry," Delores said. "But it's not."

"O.K.," I went on, finishing the coffee. "I didn't catch Ressner. So you got me on Talbott's trail. Ressner is crazy but he's no fool. Why would he call Talbott and give his right name? He was acting like a man who wanted to get caught, and catch him I did at the Manhattan Bar. More guesswork now. Ressner got Talbott in the back room. You waited for me, knowing I'd take the bait again. I'm not too bright and easy to hook. You hustled Ressner out after stabbing Talbott. My bet this time is that Doc Winning did the killing and blasted me when I went through the door. You all killed Grayson for the money you girls will inherit. You killed Talbott for one or two reasons I don't know about. I'll give you one good one. With Talbott's murder filling the newspapers, Grayson would be lost in the shuffle. But I was still on the trail, and I might foul things up, so you cooked up the wild turkey chase to Fresno, pinched my wallet—I'll give that one to Delores who probably followed me in the Packard—and let me walk into the Winning Institute while Daddy went nuts with another shot at Mae West and this morning's mess with Cecil B. De Mille. I tell you he is one inept madman, but my guess is that he's probably harmless or was until Doc Winning put a bug in his ear and sealed the ear. Last idea, you would have been happy if Jeffrey Ressner met with an accident while rampaging after celebrities. He almost did have that accident. If he got caught, you'd get your hands on him fast and see to it that he didn't say anything embarrassing. But even if he did, no one was likely to believe him.

"It wasn't a bad scheme," I concluded. "Just too complicated. Too many holes. Too much ad-libbing. Believe me, it's the dumb ones who are hard to catch. They just do it and run. Then they keep their mouth shut and may never get caught. It's you cutie pies who stick your feet in the frosting."

"I never wanted Jeffrey to be hurt," Mrs. Grayson said earnestly.

"None of us want Mr. Ressner hurt," said Winning, fumbling for his pipe, finding it, and putting it nervously into the corner of his mouth. "I'm afraid, Mr. Peters, you just created, as you said, a ghost story. You certainly have no evidence for any of this."

"Right," I said, standing up. "I can't prove any of this, but with what Ressner is probably saying right now—"

"He's psychotic," said Winning, removing his pipe. "Any psychiatrist will confirm his condition. As you just said, no one is going to believe him."

"But they'd probably believe me," I said. "I wonder what happens when I tell my tale to my brother the Homicide cop and he takes each one of you into a little office for some coffee and a chat. You'll start stepping all over one another's story, and my bet is the poor widow will crack before the first cup is cool. I've got about two bucks in change I'll bet on it, and I know a bookie who would give about eight to one against Mrs. Grayson after looking at her for thirty seconds."

"I think you underestimate us and overestimate yourself, Mr. Peters," said Delores, walking over to calm her mother, who was close to hysteria.

"Maybe. Why don't we just wait and see? I'll leave you three here to talk it over." I made a move to the door, but Winning's voice stopped me.

"Wait. Peters, I think I have something that will show you how wrong you are, that will convince you."

I turned to look at him, at all of them, and waited. He moved quickly into the back of the house, fumbled in one of the rooms, and came in holding a .38 automatic.

"Just stand still, Peters, while we consider our next step."

Mrs. Grayson was weeping now, and Delores moved to her side.

"The next step is obvious. You kill him, and we bury him in the desert," she said.

"All right," sighed Winning.

"Two questions for a dying man?" I asked.

"Very fast ones, Peters, this is upsetting Mrs. Grayson," he said.

"Sorry. How good was my story?"

"So-so," he admitted. "A few details were off, but very close. Your second question?"

"Is that my gun?"

"It is," he said. "Now Delores, I suggest you take your mother to her room for a while." Delores and Jeanette obeyed and left Winning and me alone.

"That gun makes a big noise when it goes off," I said, taking a step toward him.

"There's no one around to hear it for half a mile, and there's nothing at all unusual about shooting at prairie dogs at night," he said.

I took another step toward him and he raised the gun to fire. With my next step he did fire but nothing happened. The step after that I was in front of him and threw a punch that came from the floor. He pulled the trigger again as he fell. The bullet took off through the window and into the night. I kicked the gun out of his hand and he rolled over moaning and holding his chin.

"I think it's broken," he moaned.

"We can only hope," I said, going through his pockets and finding my wallet. "No bullet in the first chamber," I explained. "Never is. That's the trouble with being an amateur."

I made a long-distance call to Phil and invited the family back into the living room to wait for the state police. They came in about twenty minutes and led us all out after I turned the gun over to them. Phil had called, and I was sure I'd be spending a night in the lockup at the worst. I didn't know what would happen to Winning and the Grayson girls. I didn't care.

CHAPTER 17

The stitches came out of my head three days later, the morning Phil told me that Winning and the Graysons were being booked for murder. The case was pretty good if not perfect. If Mrs. Grayson didn't take back her confession, they'd all do a lot of hard time.

The story had made the first pages of papers all across the country, primarily because Richard Talbott was one of the victims. The double murder shared space with the Japanese taking of Corregidor and the Russian counteroffensive.

There was no thank-you note from Anne for the hat, but I hadn't expected one. There was no thank-you note from Arnie either when I collected on four overdue bills, one of them going back to 1939. Barely veiled threats and, in the case of the 1939 bill, the casual showing of my shoulder holster had done the trick. The guy was a close-to-the-ground mutt who owned a hot dog stand in Tarzana. If he had given me trouble, he would have discovered an empty holster. I had hocked my .38 at Wiley's Pawn shop on Vine when the police returned it to me. With the five bucks I got for it and the eighteen left in my wallet when I got it back from Winning in Plaza Del Lago, I had enough to pay back Rosie and eat, especially with a free meal with my brother's family.

I had dinner with them in North Hollywood on Saturday. Ruth was a better cook than Mrs. Plaut's Aunt Jessica, but I had to spend part of the time looking out for my niece, Lucy, whose favorite game was to sneak up behind family members, yell "Surprise," and whollop them with whatever was at hand, a doll, an old lock, a toy gun. She had started the game as a baby and was having trouble breaking the habit at the age of almost three.

"President's eating fresh fruit and cutting back on desserts with sugar," Ruth said, apologizing for not having made my favorite chocolate pudding pie. I peeled a navel orange and ate it, watching for Lucy and keeping a hand ready to defend my not-completely-healed head.

Phil said nothing. Well, almost nothing. At one point he asked to have the stew passed to him.

After dinner the boys and I left. I thought Phil wanted to say something, but he didn't. Ruth said they had to be home by eleven, and out we went.

I couldn't find much to see, and I wanted to play it safe, so we saw *My Gal Sal* with Rita Hayworth and Victor Mature.

"I wish I could do that," Nat said when we got out of the show.

"What?" asked his brother, shoveling in the last greasy drops of popcorn.

"Make my whole scalp go up and down like Victor Mature when he's thinking. Can you do that, Uncle Toby?"

I tried and failed and then asked the boys casually how their father had been in the last week or so.

"Like always," said Nat. "Busy. We were supposed to go to the park last week for a picnic, but he was chasing crazy killers again. He keeps catching them but there's always more."

Dave dropped the empty popcorn box in a wastebasket, and we all climbed in the front seat of the car.

"Are you going to be cops?" I asked.

"I think I'll be a private cop so I can shoot rat-faced hoods like you do," Nat said seriously."

"The problem is they usually shoot me first," I said.

"I'll think about it," he said. "Dave will probably be a comedian in dives around the city and Lucy will be a has-been."

"You've got it all worked out," I said.

"It pays to plan ahead," Nat said, punching his brother in the shoulder for no reason I could see.

On the morning the stitches came out, I got a check in the mail from my last client, Emmett Kelly the circus clown. He invited me to drop in on him if I came East. I read the letter over a taco at Manny's and figured out that I now had enough money to pay my fifteen bucks rent to Mrs. Plaut and ten to Jeremy for the office. I gave Arnie twenty more bucks toward the now-repaired Ford and still had enough to eat for another week or two if I drove very little and made no further moves in my so-far-unsuccessful assault on Carmen the cashier at Levy's Grill.

So, on the morning the stitches came out I went over to the Hope Street YMCA after setting up a handball game with Doc Hodgdon, the sixty-six-year-old orthopedic surgeon, who as usual barely worked up a sweat in disposing of me 21–4, 21–9. I slumped to the locker room with Hodgdon looking for someone else to take on before he went back to manipulating the spines of the wretched.

I went back to my boardinghouse and called the Winning Institute, where I was informed that the institute was undergoing a name change. Henceforth, the place would be called the Fresno Institute for Mental Research. Dr. Vadergreff was now in charge, though Dr. Winning was eventually expected to return.

In ninety-nine years to life, I thought, and asked for special permission to speak to Sklodovich.

"I'm sorry," the woman on the other end said, "there is no one in the institute with that name."

"Cortland," I said.

"We do have such a patient," the woman said, "but I'm afraid you cannot speak to him. There are strict orders—"

"Let me talk to Dr. Vadergreff," I jumped in. "Tell him it's Toby Peters. I don't care where he is or what he is doing."

The line clicked off. For a second or two I thought she had cut me off, but the line clicked back on, and I recognized Dr. Vadergreff's voice through his first cough.

"Yes, Mr. Peters," he said in his best doctor manner.

"I want to talk to Cortland," I said. "If I don't, I'll initiate a lawsuit against your little castle for kidnapping me. It might not hold up, but with the publicity you've already had, you'll have to pack up the place stone by stone and move it to Canada."

"I see," he said. "I'm not sure it would be good for Mr. Cortland."

"I have great respect for your opinion," I said, "but at the moment I think you should shove it in a tin can and get Cortland on the horn."

The phone went down hard, and I looked down the stairs to watch Mrs. Plaut slowly rising toward me, her glasses firmly planted, her eyes narrow, a pile of papers under her arm. I turned toward the phone as she moved behind me and pretended not to see her. I kept saying "uh huh, huh uh" to a dead phone until Cortland came on.

"Haven't talked on a phone for four or five years," he said.

"How's it feel?"

"Tense," he said, "Already feel that there's time and space to be filled, and if I stop talking we'll be wasting telephone air or something."

"I know how you feel. I'm sending you a dozen oranges this afternoon. Anything else you want? Sure you don't want me to work on getting you out of there?"

"Hell no," he said emphatically. "People are getting killed out there. They tried to keep it from us, but Dealer found out about Dr. Winning. They say Ressner is coming back here. Is he?"

"If he wants to," I told him. "It looks like there may be plenty of money to pay his way when the Grayson estate is settled. Of course that might take a few centuries, but the court will probably agree to use Grayson's money rather than the state's."

"Good," said Cortland. "I like Ressner. Quite an actor."

"Quite an actor," I agreed. "You want me to get the stethoscope, the raincoat, and the white uniform back to you?"

"No need," he said. "No need. There are plenty more here."

"How about a visit when I get enough cash together for gas?"

Now there was a pause on the other end while Sklodovich/Cortland thought about it.

"I don't think so. I think I'd feel a little awkward now that I know you're really not one of us. No offense. Sorry."

"Hey, don't apologize for everything. Remember?"

"Right," he agreed. "Thanks for the oranges."

Then the line did go dead, and I turned to Mrs. Plaut, who dumped the pile of papers in my arms.

"Very rough," she said. "Revision of the chapter on Uncle Will Parmarshall's kidnapping."

"Who kidnapped him?" I asked, taking a step toward my room, where I planned to drop the manuscript.

"No one," she said, following me and poking me with a steely elbow to get the common sense moving in my battered body. "He kidnapped Olivet Marsh back in the rush at Summter's Mill when Olivet and his gang of murderous thugs tried to take Uncle Parmarshall's barber chair."

"I'm looking forward to reading it," I said.

"Take care of it this time, Mr. Peelers, and remember, no more bodies in your room." She actually wagged her finger at me, and I nodded and pushed my door open.

Gunther was off somewhere seeing a publisher about a job, and I didn't feel like reading about Uncle Parmarshall, especially in rough form. I had some Pepsi and a Wonder Bread sandwich of tuna salad remnants and a slice of Kraft yellow.

The next step was clear, but I didn't want to take it. I'd make some calls to the not too affluent but not yet decayed hotels around Los Angeles, where I knew the house detectives to see if any of them needed some part-time help or someone to fill in while they went on vacation or had a nervous breakdown. If they had the breakdown, I could steer them away from Fresno Mental. If that didn't pan out, I could call a guy named Buddy who did skip-tracing in Sacramento and take on some of his dirty jobs for a percentage. Before I did that, however, I'd spend another day in

my office waiting for the mail or the phone to ring.
Everything was fine on the drive down to Hoover. The car was
running; my watch wasn't. The radio was playing, but just two
stations, the gas gauge was jumping all over the place, and my
bumper was back on along with both headlights.

I parked behind the Farraday, locked the car, looked around for
marauding bums, and went in. I saw Jeremy talking to Alice Palice
on the second-floor landing. He held a bottle of Lysol in one massive mitt and a rag in the other. Alice was speaking with passion,
and Jeremy was nodding. I couldn't make out the words, but they
made an impressive couple, minimum of 450 pounds of muscle
between them.

In the lobby of the offices I shared with Shelly Minck I stopped
to examine the dusty picture of a decaying tooth. I wondered what
would happen if my teeth went bad. Would I turn to Shelly for
help or kill myself? I went through the reception-room door, pushing one ratty waiting chair back where it belonged and saw Shelly
talking to a woman in the chair, who seemed to want to leave. She
was a little, dark woman with brown frightened eyes, clutching a
colorful beaded handbag to her chest.

"See," Shelly beamed, removing the cigar from his mouth to
face me. "That ad has been great. People from all over. I think this
woman came all the way from Juarez to see me."

"No," said the woman. "No. *No quiero que usted trabaja sur
mis dientes.*"

"See," cackled the dentist, holding her back with a fat paw.

"She says she's not here for you to work on her teeth," I
explained.

"Sure she is," he said, touching her head to calm her and getting his ring caught in her hair. "She's just frightened. Those teeth
need work. Tell her I take pesos but I make my own exchange
rate."

"*Que quiere, señorita?*" I said.

At that point the woman told me in panicked Spanish that she
had seen Shelly's ad and had recognized him as the dentist who
had ruined her husband's bridgework ten years earlier in Yuma.
She had come to demand her money back.

I explained to Shelly, who put his right hand to his chest as if he
were going to pledge allegiance to the flag or have a heart attack.

He did it with all the sincerity of a kid caught with his hand in the fudge.

"I've never seen this woman or her husband in my life," he gasped. "Tell her to get out immediately. Vamoose."

"How do you know you've never seen her husband?" I asked reasonably as Shelly tried to pry the woman out of the chair. Now she didn't want to go.

"I have, as you know, an excellent memory," he grunted, pulling at her and pausing only to marvel at her determination.

"Mi esposo se llama Martin Gutierez," she said to me.

The name shot through Shelly like a double dose of Ex-Lax.

"Oh, no," he said. "Out."

"Recuerda," she insisted. *"Mi esposo es un hombre muy grande."*

"She says," I told Shelly enjoying the scene, "that her husband is a big man."

"Muy grande," she said, wrestling with Shelly for her purse.

"Very big," I translated.

He let go of the purse, wiped his sweating brow with the corner of his dirty smock, and gasped, "How much? How much does she want?"

"Cuanto?" I asked with my most pleasant smile.

She told me but I didn't need to interpret.

"Fifty dollars?" he groaned. "Never."

"Suit yourself, Shel, but I think she'll come back some time with her husband, and it'll cost you a lot more than fifty to move to another office. Besides, your home address is in the phone book."

"Sneaky Mexicans," he snorted, going to the drawers in which he kept his tools, old X rays, and a small box with cash. He grumbled with his back turned, found what he was looking for, closed the drawer, and returned with some bills. He handed them to Mrs. Gutierez, who counted them and shoved them into her beaded purse with a smile.

"See those teeth?" Shelly said with the trace of a grin. "They'll be dropping like Nazi's in Russia in weeks, and I won't lift a finger to help her."

Mrs. Gutierez thanked me and went out the door as fast as she could move.

"Damned ad," growled Shelly, ambling over to pour himself coffee. "I'm going to pull it."

"How many Gutierezes are there out there, Shel?"

"None. He's the only one. A slight error in judgment. A slip. Everyone is entitled to one slip in an illustrious career. Even Joe Louis lost to Schmeling."

Shelly grabbed his glasses just as they were about to slip from his nose and slopped coffee on his smock in the process. It joined a collage of other stains.

The outer door to our office opened and someone knocked at the second door.

"Yeah," yelled Shelly and then to me, "it's probably the South Pasadena Fire Department coming for my ears."

"You treated the South Pasadena Fire Department and—"

"It was just a routine checkup," he said. "How was I to know . . .? Toby, I'll give you te—five bucks to protect me from sore losers for the next week till the ad dies."

"Cash in advance," I beamed. He went into his pocket, fished out a five, handed it to me, and looked at the door, which was opening.

A reasonably well-dressed couple in their early sixties stepped in. The woman was in front. The man behind was holding his swollen jaw.

"Dr. Minch?" she said, looking at me and Shelly, who was hiding behind me grasping his coffee cup in two hands.

"Minck," I corrected. "That's him."

"We read your ad in the paper. Joseph has a terrible toothache."

Shelly handed me the coffee cup as he pushed past me and hurried forward to lead Joseph to the dental chair.

"You are fortunate indeed," he said. "I've just had a cancellation."

I poured the coffee into the sink, deposited the cup, and went into my office and called Levy's to see if Carmen had checked in yet. She hadn't. I said I'd call back. I had five bucks. Maybe I could talk Carmen into a couple of late-night tacos and a swing-shift movie. Laurence Olivier was playing in *The Invaders*.

That reminded me. I had planned to take my nephews to another show when I had the cash, if my sister-in-law Ruth would let me.

I called, looking out the window to see if my car was safe. It was. Ruth answered on the second ring. I could hear two-year-old Lucy in the background saying, "Why? Why? Why? Why?"

"Ruth, it's me, Toby."

"I know. How are you?"

"I'm O.K.," I said. "I thought I'd take the boys to a movie Saturday night. No horror movies. I promise."

"It's all right with me," she said. "How did the Mae West business come out?"

I didn't know what, if anything, Phil had said about Mae West, and I didn't want to put my mouth where it didn't belong.

"Mae West?" I asked.

"Toby," she said, with Lucy still yelling in the background. "I can't ask him. He doesn't even know I know, but I know. I knew about it when it happened before we were married. Phil doesn't know I know."

I wished I hadn't called.

"It came out fine," I said. "Phil's—"

"I know," she said. "He is a good man, and he works too hard and cares too much and weighs too much and will have a heart attack just like your father if he's not careful, and he's not going to be careful."

"That's about it," I agreed.

"Come over for dinner first on Saturday and then you can take the boys," she said. "Try to be here by five."

She hung up and I went through the mail. Five letters. Two were junk mail, one selling magic supplies and the other subscriptions to cartoon magazines. The third was from the Internal Revenue Service. I put it in the top drawer with the forms I still hadn't filled out. The fourth letter was a hand-written thank-you note from Cecil B. De Mille. It was nice and simple, just "Thank you. C.B."

The last letter was the mystery. I turned it over two or three times and looked at the return address in the corner. There was no doubt. The address was not off some copying machine. It was marked personal and for me. I pulled out my Tahitian letter opener and carefully slit the top, wondering who was writing to me from the White House in Washington.